"TESS, YOU TASTE OF FRESH APPLES AND SWEET-est honey," Ian murmured.

His hard-soft mouth moving urgently on hers brought Tess to the point of mindlessness. She was stunned by the depth of her hunger, dizzy with the sensations his lips awakened in her.

"I've wanted to know the look of that mouth well-kissed," he said. "All the time you were ill, I kept thinking of it. Do you want this?" he whispered. "Do you want . . . ?" He couldn't say it, couldn't make himself ask if she wanted him.

Her head gave a jerky nod, even as her eyes looked away and her cheeks burned with shame.

"Nay, lass," he said, his palm cupping her face tenderly. "Ye're human, as am I. Ye're lovely and passionate. Dinna regret those things."

Tess stared into his glowing eyes until a tear fell down her cheek.

"Do ye wish me to leave ye, then?" he asked.

Her eyes widened in panic. She gave a minute shake of her head and took a deep breath.

"What would ye have, lass?" He had to be sure.

"You," came the whispered answer. When had she ever wanted anything so much?

WHAT ARE *LOVESWEPT* ROMANCES?

They are stories of true romance and touching emotion. We believe those two very important ingredients are constants in our highly sensual and very believable stories in the LOVESWEPT line. Our goal is to give you, the reader, stories of consistently high quality that may sometimes make you laugh, sometimes make you cry, but are always fresh and creative and contain many delightful surprises within their pages.

Most romance fans read an enormous number of books. Those they truly love, they keep. Others may be traded with friends and soon forgotten. We hope that each LOVESWEPT romance will be a treasure—a "keeper." We will always try to publish

**LOVE STORIES YOU'LL NEVER FORGET
BY AUTHORS YOU'LL ALWAYS REMEMBER**

The Editors

LORD OF
THE ISLAND

KIMBERLI
WAGNER

BANTAM BOOKS
NEW YORK · TORONTO · LONDON · SYDNEY · AUCKLAND

LORD OF THE ISLAND
A Bantam Book / April 1994

*LOVESWEPT and the wave design are registered
trademarks of Bantam Books, a division of
Bantam Doubleday Dell Publishing Group, Inc.
Registered in U.S. Patent
and Trademark Office and elsewhere.*

*If you would be interested in receiving protective vinyl covers for your
Loveswept books, please write to this address for information:*

*Loveswept
Bantam Books
P.O. Box 985
Hicksville, NY 11802*

ISBN 0-553-44285-6

Published simultaneously in the United States and Canada

*Bantam Books are published by Bantam Books, a division of Bantam Dou-
bleday Dell Publishing Group, Inc. Its trademark, consisting of the words
"Bantam Books" and the portrayal of a rooster, is Registered in U.S. Patent
and Trademark Office and in other countries. Marca Registrada. Bantam
Books, 1540 Broadway, New York, New York 10036.*

PRINTED IN THE UNITED STATES OF AMERICA

OPM   0 9 8 7 6 5 4 3 2 1

To Roberta Helmer (Christina Skye),
who taught me so much
with a few choice words of advice.
Thank you for your generosity.

And to Nita Taublib, for
her enthusiasm and insight—
the stuff that makes it work.

ONE

The mist rose from the sea in curling wisps, touching the two figures at the rail of the ferry. Separated by only a few feet, the man and woman seemed worlds apart.

Watching them, Angus pulled the heavy work gloves from his hands and breathed deeply of the power that flowed through him like a current. From childhood he'd been what the Scots termed "fey," or one of the "knowing."

It didn't always happen upon command, nor did it stay away from him when he wished. It was like a wild thing, with a life of its own. And for those who believed, there was a creed. *The knowing* had never yet harmed a soul, and, God willing, it never would.

Now, in this time, at this moment, he had only to look at those two at the rail to be certain they would be important to each other. His eyes closed again, then opened. His wind-weathered face creased into a half-smile: *perhaps sommat more than important.* Then he felt the lightning flash of danger, of potential disaster, and blinked quickly, trying to see. But more knowledge would not come.

Tess listened to the soft lapping of the waves against the sides of the ferry and stared into the darkness. Though it was still early evening, it might have been deep in the night, for the only light came from the shore ahead. So close now, she thought, and her heartbeat quickened in anticipation.

Skye.

She wondered again what it was about this island that made it the only corner of the world that seemed to hold a sense of peace for her. When she was a child, her grandfather had shown her pictures of it in a book in his library, as he told her the tale of the dramatic escape of Bonnie Prince Charlie aided by Flora MacDonald. She had stared and stared at those pictures as she listened to his deep, rumbling voice. The sea colors, the green grass and pearl-gray rocks, the earth tones of winter gorse and gray-blue sky had appealed to her in a way she couldn't explain.

Over the last months her thoughts had gone back to those pictures again and again. She had even found herself at the library, searching for those stark, peaceful scenes in books. She needed this island.

Finally, she could ignore the call no longer. Despite the arguments of friends and family, Tess had stubbornly packed her bags and taken the first plane to London she could get. Once there, she made arrangements to lease a cottage on the island near Dunvegan, got a train ticket, and started the long overland journey.

She knew that the Isle was popular during the summer. However now, during the winter months, in fact until May, it would be deserted but for a few locals. Or so she hoped.

Glancing to her right, Tess reassured herself with the sight of her belongings. Not far from that pile a man leaned against the rail, staring out at the bay. At five foot nine Tess was tall for a woman, but even to her, he looked immense. He had to be at least six feet four. He wore a trench coat, collar up, so that it shielded the bottom of his face.

As he looked out into the darkness, Tess caught sight of a strong profile with a hard jaw and a wealth of dark red hair hanging to his broad shoulders. His stance was unyielding, with a tension that was almost angry.

Tough guy, she thought. Still, there was something about him that drew her glance again and again.

A few minutes later the burly ferryman who had helped with her luggage came close. Tess caught the scent of peppermint. "Have you someone waiting for you at Kyleakin then, miss?"

Tess gave a slow shake of her head. "But I was told that there would be a bus to Dunvegan."

"At this hour? Och, but that's only in season, miss." The man frowned. He looked ancient, but he had the solid strength of one who had done physical labor all his life. At her first sight of his rough-hewn face and gnarled, reddened hands, Tess had instinctively trusted him. "Of course, you can probably find someone to give you a lift." Angus chuckled at her horrified expression. "Ye might get the taxi to come out from Dunvegan or Portree, but it would mean an hour's wait in this wind." He looked behind her and suddenly lit up. "Hold on a minute now."

Well, she shouldn't be surprised to be in such a mess, she decided. No one had ever accused her of efficiency. She watched in dismay as the ferryman walked up to the man at the rail with the auburn mane of hair. A few words passed between them, and she saw the big man stiffen. He seemed to hesitate before he finally gave an abrupt nod. The ferryman quick-stepped back to Tess.

"The laird'll be happy to give you a lift to Dunvegan. 'Tis his own destination."

"Oh, I couldn't." She shook her head and took a little stumbling step backward.

The ferryman reached for her elbow to steady her. "Well, it's the laird or a taxi, miss, and you've no guarantees on the taxi." The man's ruddy face fell into the crinkles of a reassuring smile. "Ye've no need to worry about the laird, miss, for all the publicity these last months. I've known him since he was but a wee lad. He'll get ye there safe and sound. We do for one another on the Isle, ye'll find."

When she looked back at the big man, "the laird," it was to see him already loading her things into his car. She bit her lip and gave a short sigh of defeat. It seemed as if, indeed, she had no choice.

Ian MacLeod was not at all pleased to have been commandeered as chauffeur for a helpless tourist. He swore to himself that if she asked for an autograph, he would leave her by the side of the road.

The day had been rough enough with the long drive after the doctor's incessant prodding and testing. Then he had the long drive back. Cursing under his breath, he piled the woman's things into the trunk of the car and glanced over to her place at the rail, taking in the bulky raincoat and the shapeless rain hat that covered most of her face. He packed away her tent and wondered grimly if the woman had even the slightest notion how to pitch the contraption. After he stuffed away canvas and easel, he knew she had to be the new Fergusson tenant. They had said she was an artist, but she looked to be another of those frumpy schoolmistress types who watched birds and cooed over the sheep as she did watercolors of the loch. Probably taught papier-mâché sculpture to overprivileged adolescent girls. He only hoped she wasn't one of the chatty ones.

He wasn't in the mood for a coze.

Tess felt the movement of the ferry as it began to dock. Tightening the scarf around her neck, she pushed away her shyness and walked up to the man.

"It's very kind of you to give me a ride," she told him in a halting voice that revealed her discomfort. She'd never been very good at accepting favors, especially from strangers.

" 'Tis naught," he said gruffly.

Tess looked at the man more directly when she realized that his face was half-turned from her. Perhaps he was only shy, but her limited experience of the Scots was that they were so friendly, they would start a conversation simply to pass the time, overcoming even *her* shyness.

"My name is Tess Hartley," she introduced herself, when he made no move in that direction. She drew the line at getting into a car with a stranger whose name she didn't know. Clutching her shoulder bag to her chest, she bobbed forward, trying to see his face.

"Ian MacLeod," he answered abruptly. "And I am sure that Angus has already informed you that I am quite harmless, despite my . . . appearance."

Puzzled, Tess looked more closely, for the man

was finally facing her directly. First, she saw the brilliance of green eyes, deep as emeralds. Then her glance fell to the flattened cheekbone and red scars extending from temple to jawline on his right side. Without those injuries his would have been one of the most handsome faces she had ever seen. He had a wide brow, a perfect Roman line of a nose, and a triangular jaw.

But his mouth was a sin. Full and sculpted, it was the kind of mouth that caused women to make fools of themselves.

Because he seemed to be waiting for some horrified reaction, Tess simply held out her hand. "How do you do?"

He stared at her for a moment in disdain and disbelief, then turned to the driver's door, saying, "We'd best be on our way."

Tess was left with her hand outstretched and no choice but to follow her belongings, despite the man's rudeness. Well, after another hour, she'd never have to see the big jerk again, she reassured herself.

"The Fergusson cottage?" he demanded gruffly as she closed the car door.

"How did you know?" Tess turned toward him in astonishment. From this angle she could see what he must have looked like before the incident that scarred him.

"Tim Fergusson told my man he had some artist daft enough to come to the Isle for the winter who'd be taking his cottage." He knew as he spit out the words that he used the insult to keep her at a distance. His property adjoined the Fergussons', and the last thing he wanted was a scruffy schoolteacher asking him in to tea of an afternoon. Not that he could really see *what* the woman looked like under all that swaddling.

Tess turned sideways toward m'Lord Arrogance. "Perhaps it would be better if I didn't inconvenience you, Lord MacLeod. . . ." she began, with mock deference to his title.

"Ye're goin' to make a fuss now, are ye?" he said in a low voice, his brogue thick with anger. "Has my face put the little *artist* miss off her supper?"

That got her temper up. "On the contrary my . . . lord," Tess returned in an even voice. "It would take more than a few red scrapes to put me 'off my supper.' However, your manners do leave a great deal to be desired, and I'm not at all certain I care to subject myself to them."

Laird Ian MacLeod had been termed many things in his thirty-nine years—womanizer, mischief-maker, heartless rogue, and even devil, but he had never before been accused of having poor manners. Something close to a smile curled his lip.

"Perhaps ye're right," Ian finally announced. "But ye're here now," he grumbled, spoiling the semblance of an apology. He changed gears as if that settled matters.

Tess stared in amazement at this further confirmation of the man's arrogance. When he said no more, she realized that "the laird had spoken." She raised one dark brow in wry amusement and turned back to the window as they moved onto the main thoroughfare. Soon they left the village behind, and the road began to twist and turn with the coastline. The sky was sheer black, with no lights on the road. Tess gripped her hands on the purse in her lap and stared at the beams of the headlights.

She tried to pretend she was still on the train.

As each mile passed beneath his wheels, Ian felt worse for his rudeness. In truth, his mother would have boxed his ears for displaying such a lack of hospitality. But he'd been through hell today, and sweet Aileen wasn't here to see, so he simply pressed harder to Dunvegan.

Suddenly, he slammed on the brakes and bellowed out his half-opened window, "Stop there, ye devilmaker!"

As they slid to a wrenching stop, he reached out to shield Tess with his strong left arm. Her hands had flown to cover her eyes, trapping his forearm against her full breasts. Her heart thudded so hard that he felt it through both their coats.

"Easy now, lass," Ian turned to her and said in a slow, sure voice, "ye're all right. 'Tis only that wee daft hound racing the countryside."

"I—I'm sorry." Tess forced herself to release her

death grip. Trying to still her shaking, she told herself that he couldn't help her. No one could help her. The past wouldn't be changed.

Sending a last, measuring look to the trembling woman beside him, Ian got out of the car and went to where a half-grown dog crouched in his headlights. He gathered the dog into his arms like a wayward lamb and moved swiftly, opening the back door, placing him gingerly on the backseat.

"Is he hurt?" Tess asked breathlessly. Turning to look, she saw a shaggy lump with bright eyes.

Ian grumbled and patted the black-and-white fur, checking over bones, searching for injuries or the pupil dilation of shock. The only movement was that of the dog's tail, back and forth in a happy swath. Soon the pup had squirmed onto his back, waving his legs in excitement, hoping to have his belly rubbed.

"Och, ye grand faker!" Ian admonished gently. "Did they turn ye out then, or did ye run off?"

Tess gave a shaky smile, reaching out to let the eager scamp have a sniff of her fingers. The sniff was quickly followed by an ingratiating lick. A giggle escaped her, and Ian's head jerked up. He stared, astonished at the carefree beauty of the sound. Then he continued to stare when the dog made a grab for the woman's shapeless rain hat. Long, lustrous black hair fell like a satin curtain around her shoulders, and she giggled again.

"So you know this little guy?" Tess asked Ian,

thinking that the man's scars were hardly visible in the shadows as he bent to the open car door.

Ian was equally amazed at the change he saw from dowdy schoolmistress to dark-eyed siren in a sack of a coat. Her hair was long and straight, parting at a widow's peak. Her eyes were deep blue with brows like wings across her forehead, and her mouth was soft and red, even without the aid of cosmetics.

"Aye, that I do," he answered, recalled to the reality of his own appearance even as he remembered the feel of her when she had grabbed his arm against her. She'd been soft and firm, all at once. Female to his male. Clearing his throat, he snatched the woman's hat from the dog and slammed the door. When he got back into the driver's seat, he said, "This beast is the worthless product of centuries of prizewinning sheepherders." Ian allowed himself one sideways glance at the woman beside him as he pushed the hat into her hands. "The animal won't be taught to herd."

"Well, give him time," Tess protested instinctively. "He's still so young. . . ."

"A year now, and he doesna take to it." His deep, expressive voice had turned flat with concern. Tess only heard that it had turned flat. "A crofter will take six or eight months with a dog to know its character. This one likes to *play* with the sheep, when he isna runnin' over the land, creatin' havoc. They so disparage him, they've given him no name but Dog."

And innumerable curses, he thought to himself. "His future is . . . well, doubtful, at best."

Tess turned to look again at the small animal panting happily, then she looked at the obviously embittered man beside her in the darkened car. "They wouldn't hurt him?"

"These people work for a living, miss," he announced with a certain condescension.

Tess decided that he said "miss" when he wanted to say "stupid."

"They are crofters who depend upon the wit of their dogs. They can ill afford a toy animal about the place when they need to feed and clothe their children."

Tess took a moment to absorb that. Her hand reaching back to the wiggling mite, she asked softly, "Who can we find to take him?"

Ian sighed angrily. "M'self, I fear."

Tess didn't think this harsh man would be good for a wild spirit. He had something boiling deep, something that needed therapy—or a good kick in the pants. She knew which one she'd rather he received.

"And what do *you* do with worthless puppies, Mr. . . . Lord MacLeod?"

There was a moment of black silence. Then he glanced over at her and gave a haughty stare. "In Scotland the title used is 'Laird.' And perhaps you'd like to tell me your suspicions, miss?"

"*Ms.* Hartley," she told him again. "And my suspi-

cions are that a man who speaks so casually of destroy-
ing a puppy—"

Ian straightened and sputtered with indignation,
"I never did!"

"You sound as if you do it or condone it, Your
Lairdship," Tess glared at him. " 'They can ill afford
to keep a toy animal about the place'—your words,
not mine."

"I do neither, for your information." Ian steamed.
The woman had made him sound like a bloody savage!
"And if I've ever met a more presumptuous, uncon-
trolled busybody of a woman, I canna think when!"

Tess ignored his further rudeness and turned fond-
ly to the backseat. "*I* think you should be called Duke.
You certainly outclass a mere *laird* in temperament."
Tess didn't know what it was about this man, but he
definitely lit her ornery streak. "Duke. Do you like
that?" She watched his black-tipped tail wag happily
in answer. "All right," she said, pulling the wet,
pointed nose close to her to place a smacking kiss
beside one bright brown eye.

"Duke?" Ian turned his good side to her and
scowled his reproach. "This piece o' mischief?" A
huffing sound came from him. "He's to outrank me
in m'own house, and I'm to live with it for fifteen years?
Some o' the beasts live to be twenty or more!"

Tess grinned and captivated the man with the
sweetness of it. "He's your dog," she said, looking
back at the smiling hairy monster. "Call him what you

will. I just thought it would be close enough to what he's been called before that he might recognize it."

Ian started the car again and turned back to the road, grumbling reluctantly, " 'Tis an idea."

By the time Tess had settled back in her seat, they came through what looked like a small village. She could see the gleam of the loch and lights from many of the structures that lined the road.

"Dunvegan," announced her surly guide. "The Fergusson cottage is a way up the road." He turned a corner and drove up the hill for another mile before pulling into the short driveway of a darkened structure. Tess released an audible sigh at the idea of being out of the car.

Ian frowned. "Ranald was to start the coals and lights for you."

"Ranald?"

"My man," Ian answered, "but he factors for a few others here, as well."

"Factors?" Tess shook her head, and he stared at the dark ribbon sheen of her hair. "I don't understand."

"He looks after this and that for some of the property owners. He must have been slowed down by another job." He grunted. "I will see to you m'self."

Tess felt her brows rise and fall in surprise. "Really, that's quite all right," she said hastily. "They've told me where to find the key."

But the man wasn't paying her the slightest bit

of attention, only dragging her things from his trunk while Duke chased excited circles around him. Watching him stuff the tent and easel under his arm, Tess decided that the laird would have his way, regardless. Then, as she saw the uneven steps he took to the front door, she suddenly realized he had a limp.

Face red, she rushed forward and tried to grab the handle of her suitcase, saying, "Here, let me get that."

But her offer only made him stiffen and spit out, "Get the key, woman, if ye're so anxious that I dinna drop yer things."

Tess snatched her hand back as if he had burned her, indignation rising once more. "I'm sorry."

"I need none o' yer help!" he told her, placing his load on the front step. He reached down to flip up the corner of the mat and retrieve the key. Still ignoring her, he moved her things inside.

Tess was so angry by then, she stomped back to the car and got the last small suitcases. When she stalked into the softly lit hallway, she looked left and saw the man bent to the fireplace. "Thank you very much for the ride!" She slammed the cases to the floor. "I'm sure I'll be fine now."

He merely looked over his shoulder with a glint in his eye. When had a MacLeod ever resisted a challenge? "Is that my dismissal then? Not even the offer of a cup of tea. They've interesting ways of expressing thanks in the States."

"I beg your pardon." Tess fumed, thinking that the man had the most colossal nerve. If he was on the other side of her door, she would greatly enjoy slamming it in his face. Instead, she asked in her sweetest voice, "Would you care for a cup of tea before you go, Laird MacLeod?"

Perversely, Ian accepted her offer, saying, "Aye, that I would. Thank you." He did it knowing she was dying to get rid of him, just to see the spark of temper in the deep blue of her eyes. "I'll fetch more coal from the bin while you put the kettle on. Mind the water boils, now, lass, none of your Yankee tea that's naught but tepid water and a bag." He stood, enjoying the frustrated surprise on her face, and finished by saying, "Think you can find the kitchen by yourself, miss?"

Tess set her jaw and carefully returned his mocking smile. "It's entirely possible." Since this is a seven-room cottage, she thought nastily, not Edinburgh Castle! She hung her coat in the hall, grateful for the warmth of her thick sweater.

Because he was being such a pain, she made a grand production of the tea, setting out doilies and biscuits she discovered in the cupboard. When she returned with the tray, she found MacLeod in his flannel shirtsleeves, Duke lying sleepily at his feet. For such a large man he moved with a fluid sensuality that surprised her. Another thing she decided was annoying. Then she darted a look his way and frowned, wondering why that should annoy her.

Sitting with him before the fire and watching his smug amusement, Tess could barely resist letting her pinkies fly through the air as she served. But as she was determined to show the big galoot how much better her manners were than those he displayed, she controlled herself.

"Milk?" she asked.

"Ta."

She assumed that was yes. "Sugar?"

He shook his head and she handed him the cup. When he made certain their fingers touched, Tess rattled the china, then lingered with her fingers pressing his to still the cup. With a start she pulled her hand away and poured tea for herself.

Ian sipped and watched her, the graceful way she moved, the self-conscious blush that colored her cheeks. He was strangely interested in this woman, not simply because of her surprising looks, which she had taken some pains to conceal, but also because he liked her quick temper. More important, he was intrigued by her lack of revulsion or pity at his appearance. But those thoughts were dangerous, and he had played games long enough. He had no intention of entangling himself with another woman. He had his own life to get back to, he decided, lunging to his feet.

"Duke!" he bellowed, and turned to her, enjoying her startled expression at his rudeness. "M'thanks for the tea and good night to you."

TWO

He saw her nearly every day. She was walking the moor or staked out on the knoll with that flimsy tent of hers half-opened as a windbreak while she sketched. The woman was always underfoot.

After the first week he noticed that Duke often walked with her. She never seemed to wear anything but baggy sweaters and pants, sometimes that sack of a coat. The disguise made him wonder again what, or whom, she was hiding from.

Tess saw him too. He hadn't told her that his house was just across the road and down. Actually, it was a bit like a manor house, but not as fine as she thought a laird's residence would be.

For a man with his sense of consequence, she thought it strange that he kept geese and a pig and cared for a small band of sheep that Duke happily terrorized. He also seemed to spend a great deal of time repairing the outbuildings and fences of his property. She found herself watching for him, his great shoulders straining as he carried grain or hammered posts. His limp seemed to lessen a bit each day.

It was a friendly island ritual to wave to passersby, but the most he ever gave her was a stiff nod. That bothered Tess not at all. She was more than used to artistic temperament and had no interest in the great man's company, only in his use as a distant model for her sketches.

As for himself, Ian was busy with Ranald's chores. The older man had hurt his arm rethatching a roof in Glendale, and Ian did the work around his own property rather than have someone else on the place.

There was also his own physical therapy to be done while he waited out the time before the next operations on his face. He had never thought himself a shallow man, but the damage to his face had changed his life in almost every way he could conceive. The press had hounded "the Bonnie Laird of Skye" for weeks after the accident. But he was finally yesterday's news.

No longer did he run with wealthy friends to every corner of the continent with only minor interest paid to his own properties. At first he couldn't stomach their pity. Then he had no patience for their self-absorption and waste of talent.

At last, in his isolation, Ian began to take a real

interest in his family's estates, even the running of the castle for tourists. And his life was suddenly more interesting, more fulfilling. Everything had changed; the only dark spot was human contact.

He knew that eventually he would look normal again, with the coming operations. But his sense of self had been changed forever, and he was damned if he would bear the pity of friends or acquaintances. Even more, he was sick of the humiliation of being splashed across the papers of Europe as an object of pity.

There would be time enough to face the world and make new choices when he was whole again.

After two weeks of sketching patrons of the local grocery-post office, Tess found herself adopted by the owners, Janet and Geordie. She looked forward to their affectionate bickering and her own chair by the warmth of the stove most afternoons. This time, as she entered the store, the first words she heard were, "When did Ranald say they'd do the surgery? He'll be better after that. Ah, good day to you, Tess. How are you keeping away up there on the hill?"

Tess smiled as she always did at the homey sight of the sweet-natured, middle-aged lady shopkeeper whose sweaters looked as if they'd been pulled out of shape by fussing hands. "I'm very well, thank you, Janet. But don't let me interrupt. . . ."

"Och, we were just discussin' himself and the news about his surgery to come."

"Himself?" Tess took the bait. Rosy-cheeked Janet loved nothing more than a good gossip, and in the short time Tess had been on the Isle, she had learned more genealogy and scandals than she knew about her own relatives.

"The laird," Janet started as she handed Tess a London tabloid with a blowup of Ian's scarred face on the front page. "But didna Angus tell us you drove with the laird from Kyleakin?"

"Well, yes, but—"

"And did Angus no' tell ye the lad's story so you wouldna be afeard at the sight o' him?" Janet put her hands on her ample hips.

"Well, no," Tess answered.

"Shame to him then, leavin' you to worry and wonder on the long drive, for we know the MacLeod is no' the way he was once. 'Tis a sad tale, but he's a hero as they say, right enough." Janet poured out the entire story. It seemed that MacLeod had rushed headlong into a burning croft, saved the lives of a little girl and her mother, and was injured when he jumped through the second-story window with the child. Then he was pinned by a loose beam that had come down with him and horribly cut by window glass.

"Broke his leg in four places, he did, though wee Meggie was unscathed," Janet stated knowledgeably, receiving a nod from Geordie in his rocker near the stove. Janet's bosom buddy Elsbeth leaned against the much-polished counter and added her own clucking sounds.

With a little shiver of memory Tess thought of the cuts on Ben's body from the windshield. She made a sympathetic response as she reached toward the well-ordered shelf for a can of soup.

"He was in hospital for the longest time, and still they couldna finish because of infection in the bones. A fine shame that, so braw a lad he was. All the lasses were wild for him, don't you know," Janet went on. "Remember, Elsbeth, what a scandal that Cameron girl made of herself over him?" Her voice changed to a thrilled whisper. "Imagine her slipping into his bed, naked as the day she was born, only to learn she'd delivered herself to his lady houseguest, none other than Fiona Blair! What a carryin'-on there was over that! Some say he got engaged to Fiona just to stop the shenanigans." Janet turned to Elsbeth with one knowing brow raised high. "Darla Ramsey's niece works at the verra hospital, and she told Darla that after the bandages were removed, Fiona was in his room five minutes before she came barreling out, the engagement broken. The spoiled hussy! And himself not even out of his sickbed!"

So, the laird had a reason for his bitterness, Tess thought. But they did amazing things with plastic surgery these days. He wouldn't have to worry for long about attracting the girls again.

"Would ye fancy a bit o' beef, Tess?" Janet asked. "M'Geordie found some lovely steaks on the mainland today."

"That would be wonderful, thank you." Tess smiled at the kindness. "I'll have two." Janet and Elsbeth both looked so surprised and interested that she found herself stammering out, "So I c-can freeze one," before she thought to stop herself. Then, to distract them, she looked at the blanket Janet had just added to the collection on the shelf.

"Oh, Janet, a new one! It's so lovely." And it was. The colors were the color of soft island mist, greens and blue-grays. "They'd love these in the States, you know. You really should think of exporting them."

"Aye, lassie." Janet laughed and turned back to the register. "As soon as they come round askin'." Tess smiled back and recognized her opportunity for escape. When the door swung closed behind her, and the little bell above it rang in farewell, Tess shook her head as she thought of all the stories she could start with the slip of a word.

She was walking back to the cottage when she saw *him* again. He was waiting at her gate, wearing tight jeans, a thick, fraying sweater, and a scowl that could have frightened a stone. But Tess Hartley was no stone.

"Laird MacLeod," she acknowledged the man, displeased that he made her so uncomfortable, willing him out of her way. At the same time she studied the line of his nose and brow.

"Ms. Hartley," he answered stiffly. He noted that she had stuffed her hair under that ugly hat again. Then he blurted out his latest irritation. "I've seen your wanderings. Has no one in the village thought to warn you of the countryside, or are you simply showing off your Yankee independence?"

Tess tilted her head to one side, set her jaw, and counted to seven before she moved past him to her front door muttering, "You really are the rudest man!" So why did he draw her so strangely when she should be repelled?

"I'm no' finished with you yet, miss!" The voice came from behind her. Tess juggled her groceries and pushed the door open, then closed it after her. Unfortunately, the man simply opened the door and walked into her house. Tess whirled around, ready to give him a piece of her mind, but before she could get out a word, he went on, "As long as ye take my dog with ye, ye'll have a care, if ye please. When you go on those walks o' yours, stay to the road. You have no way o' knowin' when a mist might come up. An' take this with you!" He thrust a long carved staff into the corner near the door. "It's for feeling the ground when ye're on the peat."

"You just told me to stay on the road," Tess protested his senseless orders with a frown.

"Aye, that I did." The rude giant crossed his arms over his great chest. "But I know too well ye haven't the sense to do the reasonable thing." And with that, he turned and stamped away, calling Duke after him in an exasperated voice.

The next days brought a kind of contentment Tess had thought she might never feel again. The amber of the dying bracken and yellow gorse was a perfect complement to gray winter skies and thick green grass. She walked, with her staff, Duke, and her sketch pad, filling the pages with island life that somehow made her feel a part of the world again. She made endless sketches, lost in the romantic images of the Isle and its people.

Her days took on a new pattern then. She woke before dawn, though dawn came late in the winter. She took that dark time to plot her work, to plan what she would sketch, whether she'd beg a ride to the ruins of the old mill wheel or explore the burn that ran in a silvery stream behind her house.

Somehow her imagination had come alive again. Perhaps it was because she was doing without the kindly interference of loved ones back home, perhaps it was the isolation of her new life or the tentative friendships she was forming in the village with people who knew nothing of her fame or history.

She could sketch, but she could not paint.

She played cards with Janet and her friends on Friday nights, taught Duke a few basic commands, and, shocking even herself, she was learning to cook with the advice of the owner/chef of the local bed-and-breakfast, an Englishwoman named Betty Doon.

Then came the anniversary of the accident that had changed her world forever. Two years, and still she shivered at the thought of having to get through the day with those memories. She hadn't fallen asleep until nearly five that morning, and when she finally awoke, it was with the feeling that there was something terribly wrong. Rubbing her eyes, she realized what it was, and her chest tightened.

She got through the morning dry-eyed, attempting to sketch, then pacing. Finally, she began to feel the hot burn of tears behind her eyelids. Midafternoon, when it became too difficult to stay indoors, she bundled up and went for a walk. Though she was usually accompanied by Duke, she didn't whistle for him today. She didn't want even his company.

For the first hour she stayed on the road, but after two cars passed her with friendly waves, she slipped through a fence and wandered over a meadow, following a flock of sheep. Her mind was so filled with images of the past, with memories both sweet and bitter, that she lost track of time. Then she heard a faint bleating. Tess tried to trace the source of the sound. Turning, she finally saw the small white lamb as it struggled in the soft mud of the bog. Its mother echoed the sounds of distress and dipped her head.

Starting forward, Tess found the peat soft beneath her own feet as the cool rain began to fall. Looking up, she realized that it must be after four, close to sundown, and she was still far from the road to home. Worse, she had forgotten MacLeod's staff.

When he found her, Tess was unconscious, trapped in the bog almost to her waist. Ian would never have found her at all if it hadn't been for Duke. They weren't more than a half-mile from the house, but the daft animal kept running toward the marshy bog, no matter how many times he was called to heel. Exasperated, Ian finally had followed.

At the first sight of her his heart thundered in his ears, for she was covered in mud, her face deathly pale. He reached out to touch her cheek and found her skin icy cold. By the time he dragged her from the bog and got her back to his house, it was dark, and a winter gale had started.

Once inside his bedroom he laid her down on the coverlet and left her there long enough to start the water in the tub. When he returned, he gave her a quick assessing glance.

Her hair hung in a wet tangle over one shoulder.

Her eyes were closed, the lashes long and spiky. High cheekbones, the skin pale as cream contrasted with her full red mouth. It was the only bit of color in her face.

Moving as fast as he could, Ian stripped her, ignoring her murmurings. By the time he was down to her damp pink lace bra and panties, his hands had slowed in shock. Lying before him was the most incredible body he had ever seen. Voluptuous, perfect, it was the fantasy of any male past puberty.

Even spotted with mud, her skin had the gleam of creamy satin. Visible through the pink lace, her breasts were high and full, almost too large for her slender build. Her ribs tapered to an impossibly small waist, then there was the surprise of her full, womanly hips. The sight of her actually made him blush like a boy, even as it aroused him.

A crash of thunder brought him back. The woman had a high fever, and Hamish, the island doctor, took his weekends on the mainland. Ian would have to keep her in stable condition until morning. Hypothermia was his greatest enemy. He had to warm her, and quickly.

He stripped the rest of her things away, only to find himself once more distracted by her rounded feminine thighs and the dark triangle of curls at the juncture of her legs. Then he saw the gooseflesh that pebbled her skin.

Swiftly, Ian lifted her into his arms and carried her

to the bathroom. When he lowered her into the tub, she gave an involuntary shudder and blinked, her gaze unfocused.

"Ms. Hartley?" Ian leaned down so that she could see his face. "Tess?"

"The lamb, she's safe, with her mother," she whispered. Her eyes were so dilated, they seemed almost blue-black.

He watched as they blinked once more and closed. Her head tilted to the side.

Making sure that she would not slip down, he grabbed the bath sponge and soaped it. He needed to get the mud off her and get her into a warm bed as fast as possible. Ian sponged her face and neck, then over her delicate collarbone. His glance slid down to her breasts. They were round and luscious, with coned nipples of a delicate coral color. He'd never seen nipples quite like them.

His mouth went dry. He could almost feel the imprint of them upon his tongue.

Ignoring the burning ache in his groin, he reached blindly for her wrist and began to soap her arm in quick, efficient motions. His thumb slid back and forth absently, and he turned her wrist to the light, wondering at what he felt there.

With a solid jolt his heart stopped, then started again in a jerky rhythm. Time slowed as his thumb brushed back and forth over the thin white lines. He reached for her other wrist and found the matching patterns. Then he swallowed hard and lowered her arm carefully back to the warm water.

A strange anger burned in him as he wondered at the dark secrets that would bring a young, beautiful woman to the brink of suicide. Had she meant to kill herself today? Had she gone out to the bog hoping she wouldn't come back?

Well, damn and be damned if he'd let it happen! Not on his Isle! His green eyes as hard as gemstones, he sluiced water over her body and quickly soaped and rinsed her hair. But he had to lean her against him to keep her from slipping down. By the time he pulled the stopper out, he was almost as wet as she. He toweled her dry with a minimum of fuss, then slipped her between the sheets and dried her hair.

He was only away from her a few moments, changing his clothes, but by the time he returned to the bed to check on her, her skin was burning hot.

Cursing in a steady stream, he got aspirin and water, holding her as she swallowed in two gulps. He could see that she was still only half-aware of her surroundings. Thinking that his first priority had to be to get rid of the fever that so often followed hypothermia, he filled a basin with cool water and grabbed the bath sponge.

Throwing back the covers, he positioned towels beneath her. Then he wet the sponge and ran it downward, avoiding those enticing nipples and sliding over her ribs, past the deep indentation of her waist.

When her hips moved restlessly, he sponged her thighs and calves. She moaned, and her knee bent sideways, leaving her open to his gaze. Her hips moved once in a slight lifting motion, and moved again as she murmured something he didn't understand.

Shocked, Ian felt the sweat break out at his temples as he watched her pretty coral nipples harden even more and her breasts begin to lift with the deep, ragged breaths she took. Her eyes were still closed, the blue veins visible, but her full, reddened lips were parted as she gave a deep sigh. The heat of her skin activated the scent of his soap, and it smelled quite different on her, sweet and faintly floral.

Ian clenched his jaw and ran the sponge over her until her skin began to cool at last. Swallowing hard, he pulled the sheet back up, covering that too-inviting body.

He had to assure himself that the cause of her semiconscious state was exhaustion. If she slipped into a coma, he wouldn't know what to do to help her. Cupping her soft cheek, Ian called to her.

"Tess," he said in a compelling voice. When she didn't answer, he gave her head a little shake. "Tess! Wake up, now!" He sighed in relief when he saw her eyelashes flutter.

She murmured, "Tired. Warm now."

"That's fine. You can sleep, just open your eyes a minute and tell me your name." He almost laughed as her face puckered in childish annoyance at the order, but he was determined. "Come on, open those pretty eyes."

Finally, she obeyed with a little huffing sound. Blinking hard at first, she tried to lift her hand to her face, but it seemed so very heavy.

"What's your name?"

"Tess. Hartley." She frowned again. "Don't you know me?"

He chuckled lightly. "Aye, that I do. How do you feel, lass?"

"Hot . . . sleepy."

"All's well then. You can go back to sleep."

"Okay," she answered simply.

After watching her for a moment, he went to pour himself a dram of whisky. He shook his head, trying to banish the memory of the beauty lying in his bed.

Why did she hide beneath bulky sweaters and baggy men's pants? He remembered the darts sewn into the waist of her jeans with thick, amateur stitches. She probably had to do that with all of her clothes. Did it have something to do with the marks on her wrists? Was she afraid of men? Was that it? Or maybe she hated them.

The devil take it! It hardly mattered what the woman's problems were. She would be gone in the morning, leaving him with only the memory of her delicious body. His task was to get her fever down, and he realized with a dark scowl, he would also need to get some liquids into her.

Over the next three hours Tess alternated between burning heat and shivering cold. He sponged her repeatedly, even turning her on her stomach to cool her back and legs. She was equally lovely from this angle, he noted, with a long, sloping back and a heart-shaped bottom he found very disturbing. He turned her over again and covered her with the comforter and three blankets. Then he forced her to take more aspirin, cups of warm tea, and glass after glass of lemon water.

Sometimes she seemed simply confused, other times completely unaware of what was happening. Through the night she moaned and sighed, struggling against things that weren't there, crying out to someone named Ben until Ian could stand it no longer and gathered her close, though he knew it was the fever. He rocked her, caressing her tangled hair. Then she began to tremble, and he made a cocoon of the blankets. He held her tight until the chills passed.

Finally, Tess sat up and shoved the covers away, moving to put her feet on the floor. Her eyes blinked as if she were trying to clear her vision.

"Ah, no, lassie." Ian rushed from the chair he had pulled to the side of the bed. "Ye mustna leave the bed." He pressed her shoulders back down.

She seemed dazed but determined, as she muttered, "Bathroom" in a frog's voice.

"Oh . . . aye," he answered, realizing that he would have to help her. "That's easy enough," he reassured her as he lifted her into his arms. It was only one more necessary intimacy, after all.

When he returned her to the bed, she was exhausted, her head lolling on his shoulder. She slept for another two hours. Sometime near dawn, she kicked the covers away once more. Ian rose and put a hand to her brow. She was warm, but nothing like before. All he could do now was sponge her down again and continue giving her aspirin. Even if he took a chance on driving through the rain and wind for the hour it would take to reach the ferry at Kyleakin, he doubted it would be running until the storm calmed.

He dipped his fingers into the glass of ice water and traced her dry lips with a sliver of ice.

She sighed and turned her head toward him. Eyes closed, she reached for his wrist, and the ice fell into her hair. Incredibly, she began to drag his arm downward to her breast. With a soft cry she pressed his palm against her.

Cheeks ruddy, his expression tortured, Ian felt the hard warmth of her nipple tightening even more against the center of his hand. He closed his eyes in an effort to regain control of himself, but the sight of her, the impatient sounds of her breathing, had driven him quickly to a realm of sexual arousal he had not felt for a long, long time.

Ian stared, completely bemused, then he closed his eyes tight again. Bloody hell, he needed air!

Determined to complete the task, he jerked his

hand away, ignoring her cry of loss. In brisk motions he sponged her hot flesh over and over, until, finally, she began to cool. He dried her with a rough towel, pleased at the healthy peach color that came to her creamy skin. Then, looking down at her, he pulled the covers to her chin and tucked them around her before he stalked into the bathroom for a freezing shower.

When he returned, he found her forehead still cool, her breathing and pulse regular at last. With a short, satisfied grunt he pulled an armchair close to the bed. He watched her pale face until she began to mutter in her sleep once more.

"No . . . Ben, help me!" she whimpered helplessly, fighting the covers. Ian sat on the edge of her bed and smoothed back the sleek dark hair from her temple. His thumbs swiped over her cheekbones, drying her tears.

"Don't leave me!" Her voice was agonized, heart-wrenching. Ian gathered her into his arms, soothing her with soft words and stroking hands. After a few minutes she seemed to respond, but as soon as he began to pull away, she would fret until he held her close again. Finally, he came up onto the bed beside her. Tess immediately turned to put her head on his shoulder, her arm thrown across his chest.

Dreams, dark dreams, haunted her. First there was the crash that had stolen Ben and their unborn child.

In slowest motion she saw it all happen again. Two headlights suddenly swerving toward them—there was no time for Ben to turn from it, no way for him to protect her. There was time only for one last tortured look from his intent hazel eyes, and she felt all of his love in that instant. Then came the crash of metal against metal, the scream of the tires, and the sound of breaking glass. Tess felt her body slam against the seat belt, and then there was nothing.

After that came another dream, one of heat so intense, she could not even cry out against it. Gentle hands were followed by cooling water on her body. At times the motions eased her. Other times those hands aroused her, pulling her back from the dream world, making her burn with a different kind of fire. Why didn't they stop? Why didn't they leave her alone? The dream came again and again. Sometimes she could see flowing hair and emerald eyes with a fierce expression; sometimes she heard reassuring murmurs.

She became aware of a warm, musky scent: the scent of skin, of man. Tess sought more of its richness, nuzzling closer until her mouth made contact with the strong cords of a masculine neck.

With only one arm free she squirmed against the tight confines of a blanket, needing to get closer. At last the blanket loosened enough that she could lie on the wide chest. The soft material of his shirt had opened, and the roundness of her breast lay against burning skin covered with a thick pelt of hair. Her fingers sought the silky waves at his nape. Her nipples hardened in pleasure, and she sighed, nearly falling back to sleep. But just as she began to doze, her fingers combed through the long, soft waves of his hair once more. Long, soft . . . long, instead of short, crisp curls!

Her eyes shot open in panic, catching sight of a strong, muscled neck and wide shoulders, a chest covered in dark red curls beneath an open blue shirt. Looking slowly upward, she saw the outlines of sculpted jaw, strong, straight nose, broad brow, and thick lashes. She saw a mouth that was full and tomcat sensual, hair of darkest red, long, thick. One side of his face was terribly scarred.

"Oh, God!" Tess cried out sharply. She pushed against the center of his hard chest with her palm, trying to rise. But she was so weak that she immediately fell back on him.

Ian woke to the feel of a struggling female he wasn't even restraining and a fiery ache in his loins. He instinctively grabbed her wrists, which served to make her lie flat against him. He looked down into deep blue eyes, seeing the confusion and embarrassment. Then his glance fell to where her flesh was pressed to his. He was acutely aware of the hard pebble of her nipple and the way her hip pressed against his arousal through the blanket. Letting his glance rise again, he saw the deep peach blush suffuse her cheeks.

"Please," she whispered hoarsely, "let me go."

His hands opened, and she rolled onto her back, pulling the blanket high.

"What . . . ?" she choked out.

"I found you in the peat bog. Actually, the dog found you." Ian rubbed a big hand over his face in a weary motion, then pinched the bridge of his nose between two fingers. "Ye had a high fever in the night. How are ye feeling?"

"Weak." She tugged on the sheet, finally managing to drag it up. She tried to smile. "Stupid."

"Aye," Ian growled, his anger growing as he woke. "That's true enough! What were ye doin' out there, so close to dark? Did I not warn ye of the danger?"

Tess looked too enticing as she leaned back against the stark whiteness of the sheets. The thought of how close she had come to serious illness or death shook him in a way he didn't like.

"I . . . lost track of time," she stammered as she pushed her hair out of her face. "And I heard this sound, a lamb." She looked up. "I had to do something. It was trapped."

"Oh, aye! A fine excuse!" Ian sat up and threw the covers off. "Ye rescue a lamb and become trapped yerself!" He turned back to scowl down at her. "An' if I hadna come along . . . if that silly dog had no' run after yer scent . . . Why the bloody hell were ye wandering there in the first place?" He was breathing hard, trying to control his emotions.

Finally, she answered, with difficulty. "It was a bad . . . anniversary for me," she said, wondering why she needed him to understand. "Two years."

Ian stilled, then bent to her and reached gently for her wrist, turning the thin scars to the light. "This kind of bad?" he asked gently. He swallowed hard as he saw the tears fill her sea-blue eyes.

She nodded and they spilled over. "I wanted to die too . . . he left me . . . they left me . . . so"—her words were strangled with something between despair and anger—" . . . alone."

With an impatient sound he leaned over to drag her into his arms. "Go on, lassie," he whispered into her soft hair, "have it out."

He was so warm, so comforting. Even his smell was comforting, and the stroking of those big hands made emotions swell until she couldn't contain them any longer. She cried until she was sobbing aloud against his shoulder.

After a few minutes he was pressing soft, calming kisses to her temple. She clutched the smooth material of his shirt in one hand and pressed closer in primal need. When she raised her chin seekingly, he touched that sinful mouth to hers, and she gave another little sob.

It was a kiss of recognition, nothing like that of a stranger. Hot and sweet, his lips moved in slow, nibbling motions and played over hers until she pressed upward, needing more contact. And for a moment, he indulged her, indulged them both. His tongue sought entrance and explored, then tantalized. His breathing became ragged, and her pulse quickened, making her dizzy. But after a few seconds Ian was the one to draw away; he wanted more than kisses, and the very strength of his need reminded him of Tess's weak condition.

He looked down at her, and she was caught by the beauty of his clear green eyes. A wave of weakness washed through her, and she sagged in his arms. If she had looked up at that moment, she would have seen the tenderness in those eyes as he lowered her to the pillows.

She napped for an hour more before a gentle touch brushed against one cheek. Her eyes felt weighted, but they finally opened and blinked. Ian stood before her, holding out what might have been an immense football jersey.

"We'll play 'dress-up' for the doctor, shall we?" He was actually smiling at her! It was a one-sided smile and a little uncertain, but it was definitely a smile. He was standing above her, maneuvering the hem of the shirt so that it would go over her head. "Want to sit up?" His warm hand supported her shoulders, helping her sit. She felt his touch echo in the lowest part of her spine, vibrating like an electric current, stirring sexual interest she hadn't believed she was capable of feeling.

Tess kept looking down, checking to see that she still held the blanket in the strategic place.

Ian guided one hand, then the other, through the wide sleeves, and Tess shivered when his fingers skimmed over the bare flesh of her arms and hands. She watched the subtle swing of his thick red hair as he leaned over her to fluff the pillows. His scent was warm and masculine. It filled the air around her.

He let his fingers skim the nape of her neck as he gently freed her hair from the collar of the shirt. He couldn't help but rub the silk of it between his fingertips, but he drew away before Tess noticed more than a slight tingling at her scalp.

The doctor was a calm, soft-tummied man named MacInnes with a crazy thatch of silver hair and matching brows. He made definitive sounds low in his throat at every stage of his examination and finally gave a little cough, signaling that he was finished.

Ian had been pacing back and forth in the hall while MacInnes examined Tess. When the door was opened to him, he came back in, an anxious look on his face.

"How is it *ye*'re feelin' now?" MacInnes let his doctor's eyes fall upon Ian and his sunken cheek.

"We're not concerned for me, Hamish." Ian strode impatiently into the room and placed himself at the foot of the bed. "Get on with it, man! How is the lass?"

Hamish MacInnes allowed himself a small grin at the vagaries of human nature. Ian was interested in something other than his own troubles. That was enough.

"The fever was a result of the hypothermia, as ye thought," the doctor stated. "Now we'll treat her for the exposure. Ye did an excellent job of nursing, Ian." A twinkle lit his gray eyes. "P'haps I'll recommend ye to the council for emergencies."

Tess watched the byplay between the two men and realized that theirs was a long relationship.

"Perhaps we'll seek a doctor to stay on the Isle the weekends," Ian threatened in a dark voice, though Hamish had been his family's doctor for forty years, and it would take more than an army to dislodge him.

Hamish looked at the man he'd known all his life and saw that he had somehow gone too far. There was more here than he'd suspected. He withdrew then, into his professional persona. "Bed rest for three to four days. This will turn to a sore throat and congestion, no doubt, though I'll leave an antibiotic. If she develops a wheeze or deep cough, ye're to call m'service immediately. She'll be weak at the beginning, from the fever, ye ken. Lots of liquids. Tie her to the bed, if need be, but keep her there. If the fever returns, call me."

"Doctor!" Tess was equally outraged at being treated as if she were invisible and at the idea of

MacLeod being given responsibility for her. "I would like to go home. I'm just across the road, and I feel fine. I can certainly take care of myself."

Dr. MacInnes scowled at her from beneath his bushy brows. He had noted the scars at her wrists. "Have ye heard of hypothermia, lassie? Do ye know you almost died?" he asked flatly. "If ye had not been found when you were, and if Ian had not known how to warm ye then treat yer fever, I don't know for certain ye would have survived." He watched that information sink in and huffed when he saw that it did. He held up the palm of one hand. "Push," he demanded.

"Wh-what?" She was bewildered, still shocked at what he had told her.

"I want ye to push against me, hand to hand." When she hesitated, he demanded, "Do it!" His great bristly brows pulled together.

So she did it. And even Tess could tell that there was no force behind her push. She tried again, with an agonized sound, but she couldn't budge him.

"Three to four days abed," Hamish diagnosed with definition. He looked at Ian. "If ye have a problem accommodating the lass, I'll inquire for a private nurse."

Ian rose to his full height. "No. There'll be no word of this, Hamish. I'll care for her, an' there'll be no talk. Ye ken?"

"Aye," Hamish answered happily. "I ken."

THREE

The second Ian returned from seeing the doctor out, Tess started to protest. "I'm going home!"

"Mm," he responded.

She struggled up on one elbow. "I mean it, Lord—Laird MacLeod—"

"Ian," he interrupted with a bob of his head.

"Ian," she corrected. "I'm going home."

"Ye heard the doctor. In only a few days ye'll be strong enough to care for yerself." Ian gathered the damp towels and muddy spread from the floor like a dutiful chambermaid, stalked to the bathroom, and tossed the lot into the hamper.

"I can't impose. If you'll just help me home, I'll arrange for a private nurse," Tess said with grim determination, closing her fists and willing strength into her spine, her whole body.

"Ye don't understand." Ian was back in the bedroom. Uncompromising, he faced her, hands on hips. "If the papers get hold of this, they won't leave either of us alone for weeks. You have no idea of the kind of things they would print about you, about me, about the two of us together. The only way to save the situation is to prevent talk. *Ye're not ill.* Ye've never been ill. Ye've never been in my house the night. Callie, the woman who cleans for me, comes the weekend. Though she's discreet, there's no need to involve her. Ye'll be home by then."

She looked up, startled by his fierce determination.

"If ye wish to repay me for saving yer life"—he paused, angry at himself, for he knew well this was nothing short of blackmail—"then ye'll be my guest. In only a few days we can forget all about it. But right now, if you call for a nurse, there will be too many stories." He added in a shameless monotone, "I'm the favorite fodder for gossip these days. I've had m'fill of reporters and whisperings in the last year, never mind that ye're too weak to be interviewing medical staff. So, ye'll stay here until the doctor tells us ye're fit, and we're both protected. Hamish knew it too. There's really no choice, lass."

Tess stared at him in disbelief. She was so used to being in complete control of her own life. "You mean you'd actually try to stop me from returning to my own house?"

"Aye," he answered. " 'Tis for the best." Then his

eyes twinkled at her. "And I make a fine chicken and barley soup."

Tess was not happy. She had never felt so helpless in her life, and the only thing she could do to remedy the situation was to sleep. Ian appeared with embarrassing regularity when she needed help to the bathroom or with her meals. Her nerves grated at the thought that he was timing her, but no sooner did she shove the covers away than he appeared to aid her. And m'Lord Arrogance had somehow taken on the demeanor of a favored servant, acting as if he lived to cater to her needs.

It made her crazy.

She hated the idea of giving up control of her life to anyone, most especially to Ian MacLeod. He was angry, imperious, opinionated, self-involved. But he was also behaving in a way that completely bewildered her. He had become an angel, she was sure. An angel in disguise, for he hadn't stopped his bullying ways, but now he used them to make sure she drank her juice, ate his oatmeal, and took her pills. He supplied her with boxes of tissue and entertained her at night with card games or sat watching TV beside her, stroking Duke's soft fur. Why? she wondered.

The sheer intimacy grated on her, although he treated her so impersonally that she could hardly mind his physical attentions, all geared for her comfort and well-being. It wasn't his fault that the better she felt, the more she began to have thoughts about his strong, beautiful body.

In the house he wore flannel shirts or soft dyed undershirts with long sleeves. Beneath those, his muscles undulated with every motion. She seemed to wait for those movements as hungry as a child for a treat.

Her body was reacting in ways that she wasn't used to, and she didn't like it a bit. Silly, she thought. It was just that she was so damned weak.

Ian held the back of her head as she sipped countless glasses of water. She became used to his touch. He checked pulse and temperature, carried her to the bathroom door, and waited without like the gentleman he had never pretended to be.

When Tess found herself sketching his profile with her finger on the coverlet, she knew she was in trouble.

"D'ye have family, or friends, ye'd like to telephone?" he asked her once. She looked puzzled. "To let them know ye're all right," he finished.

Her answer was a glimmer of a smile. "No. They've learned to let me go my own way."

"I don't think I've ever met a painter," he told her one night over a game of chess.

Tess grimaced. "One who doesn't paint . . . just now."

"No?" he asked, trying not to press too hard, though he wanted to know everything about her.

"No."

"You haven't really told me about that." His green eyes looked warmly into hers. "When you were sick, you kept calling out for someone named Ben."

Tess looked away, and an expression of such sadness came over her face that Ian wished he hadn't made her remember. He had just opened his mouth to tell her it was really none of his business when she turned to face him.

"Ben was my husband," she said quietly. "He was killed, with our baby, in a car crash."

"Dear God!" Ian said, eyes filled with compassion. "I'm sorry, Tess. I should never have asked."

"No, it's all right." She swiped at a quick tear. "It's been two years. I never talk about it. But it doesn't hurt as much as I thought it would to say the words."

"How old was the baby?" he asked gently, thinking how difficult it must have been for her to go on after that.

Tess looked at him and blinked. "She wasn't born yet. I was only six months along."

Ian gasped, reached for her hand, and squeezed it. "My hurts seem so small compared to yours."

Tess smiled at him sadly and shrugged. "Hurt is hurt." She tilted her head a bit. "They bother you terribly, your scars, don't they?"

His hand fell away, and Tess had an instant to

regret it before he answered. " 'Tis not the marks, or even my cheek. I know that will be repaired." He turned his face away. "I canna bear the look of pity, sometimes worse, when people first see me. There was a woman I was tied to—but not after this. I have to admit, I make even m'family uncomfortable. It makes me want to send m'fist through a wall." He sat back and looked at her speculatively. "But you dinna look at me that way. Why?"

"Art school, I suppose. We're all just physical shape and form, Ian. The variations make us interesting, show where we've been. There's no shame in those scars. You earned them saving two lives."

Ian looked at her differently then, thinking of the hell she had been through, thinking of the scars on her wrists. "Ye're a remarkable woman, Tess Hartley. I wonder if you know."

Tess blushed and looked down at the chessboard, uncomfortable with the compliment. It seemed very . . . personal, or maybe it was the expression on his face as he said it.

Finally, she moved her knight and looked up, grinning. "Check, Your High-and-Mightyship."

He raised a brow and studied the board, thinking of her pretty breasts, unbound, each movement outlined against the jersey she wore. He made his move. "And . . . mate, I believe, Yank."

"Devil," she muttered, her grin slipping out.

"Aye, and more," he answered cheerfully.

——————◈——————

He missed her when she went back across the road, though he knew it was time. She had become too much a part of his new life. He had found himself too eager to see her every morning, to touch her in the casual ways necessary for the kind of care she had required.

No, it was better that she was gone. After all, he reasoned, they had less than nothing in common.

Tess wandered through her cottage, picking up knickknacks and putting them down, going listlessly through her sketches, then moving to the window to stare out at his house. The end of another Saturday, she thought as she watched the tall, lean figure of Ian's housekeeper walking down the path to the road in the blue twilight.

She hadn't stopped thinking about him since she had come back home, a man so big, so strong, so hurt. She remembered the night he had kissed her and wanted more. Lighting an old-fashioned oil lamp against the darkness, she placed it on the sill, wishing its light would bring him to her. Ah, well, she thought, turning to go upstairs. Some things were meant to be, and some were not.

When Ian saw the light in the window across the road, he dropped the pitchfork and began to run in an awkward lope. His heart slammed against his chest as he told himself it couldn't have been there long or he would have seen it.

The front door opened easily, slamming back against the wall to close behind him, but he was already through to the empty kitchen, calling her name. When he didn't see her, he ran back to the stairs and took them three at a time. On the landing he saw the open door to her bedroom. Never stopping, he was through that door too, in a matter of seconds. Standing next to the bed, Tess whirled at the sound of his footsteps. She wore a towel on her head and a long peach silk robe. Her mouth was a soft O of surprise, and her cheeks were flushed.

"Tess . . ." Ian said her name once more, but this time it was a caressing sound. He gave himself a mental shake. "What is it?" he demanded. "Where's the trouble?"

"What trouble?" Her blue eyes widened in confusion.

"The lamp, lass!" He frowned in exasperation. "The lamp in the window."

"Yes," she said, coaxing more information, embarrassed to tell him that it had been only a romantic notion.

" 'Tis the signal for trouble on the Isle. Did no one tell you?"

Tess shook her head, and the towel wrapped around her hair began to fall. When she raised her hands to catch it, the belt of her robe loosened enough to reveal a deep V of cleavage.

Ian's eyes were riveted. His body hardened immediately. Tess felt the heat of that look across the room and froze. After a moment she began to tremble.

"Then there is no . . . trouble?" he asked cautiously, waiting for the second shake of her head.

Ian moved forward until he stood only inches away; he stared into her eyes with burning intensity. He reached for her sash with one finger and gave a gentle tug.

Tess was astonished, but she didn't stop him. The silk panels fell open, and her hands turned to fists at her sides. Everything changed to slow motion.

His eyes flicked down once, then back to hers as he let his finger trace a line, slowly, from collarbone to navel. There his gaze dropped. She gasped, frozen. So carefully he moved. He circled, dipped, and finally slipped lower and lower, as her breath came more quickly. Fascinated, he watched the tremors that moved just under the surface of her skin with each brush of his fingers. At last he reached the dark triangle of soft curls between her thighs. Hardly believing his own daring, he moved even closer, so that his clothing brushed her nakedness. His long fingers grazed the downy hair before parting her, finding a creamy wetness that made his own breathing ragged. He felt those beautiful nipples harden against his shirt, and his other hand moved to the base of her spine beneath the robe.

Still no words, no kiss exchanged—there was only the sound of their heightened breathing in the quiet room.

As her pink tongue darted out to moisten her full lips, her head fell back in surrender, and Ian knew he had to taste her. But first, he wanted more of her tantalizing response. He loved the feel of her heat, her wetness. He loved knowing that he could draw that response from her no matter what his face looked like; and without even a preliminary kiss or caress. He sensed her need through the very pores of his skin, in the air he breathed. How long had she been without a man?

Tess couldn't believe this was happening! She felt exposed in a way that had nothing to do with clothing. A hunger had fired her blood, and it was raging through her. Why didn't she care?

Though her eyes had drifted closed, her expression was soft and dreamlike. He watched as a flush of desire stained her skin from the tips of her breasts upward to her high widow's peak. He let his fingers trace the shape of her womanhood, finding the swollen bud that made her give a low moan of desire. Gently, carefully, he circled the flesh there, stroking lightly until she pressed herself into his hand. He smiled in satisfaction as her eyes opened and her breath came in short pants.

Oh, God! What was he doing to her, and why was she letting him? She'd never been so outside herself, so beyond her own control. It was all she could do to keep from crying out her need.

Ian slid one finger deep inside her while his thumb rubbed back and forth. He was watching her blue eyes as she cried out, convulsing around him. His movements slowed but never stopped, and her eyes soon closed again as her breasts brushed his shirt, every breath creating torturous friction.

Finally, he bent to her full, parted lips. First, his tongue traced a delicate trail along her upper lip until she shivered. Then his mouth found hers with a restrained hunger, waiting only for her response. It came with another moan, and she pressed closer still, until there wasn't even an inch of space separating them. Her fists opened, and her hands found the nape of his neck, threading through his thick hair to his scalp.

She tasted of fresh apples and sweetest honey. Intoxicating! His tongue moved into her mouth, delving for each precious flavor.

That hard-soft mouth moving urgently on hers brought Tess to the point of mindlessness. She was stunned by the depth of her hunger when she had just experienced such pleasure. The hand that had played at the base of her spine moved around to cup her breast, flicking the nipple until it ached and she arched her spine in reflex. His tongue made her dizzy; his fingers made her shiver and shake. One of her legs rose to curl around him, and he groaned aloud and gripped her hips with both hands.

"I've wanted to know the look of that mouth well kissed. After the time you were ill, I kept thinking of it. Do you want this?" he whispered against her lips. "Do you want . . . ?" He couldn't say it. He couldn't make himself ask if she wanted *him*. It would be enough that she desire the act.

She pulled away, unable to speak. Her mouth trembled as she looked into deep green eyes and hard features that revealed a stark hunger. Her head gave a jerky nod, even as her eyes looked away and her cheeks burned with shame.

"Nay, lass." His palm cupped one side of her face, turning it up so that she could see the tenderness in his expression. "Ye're human, as, I fear, am I. Ye're lovely and passionate. Do not regret those things."

Tess stared into those glowing eyes until a tear rolled down her cheek, slipping to the crevice between his thumb and forefinger. His eyes closed tight then opened again.

"D'ye wish me to leave ye then?" he asked, his voice strained.

Her eyes widened in panic, and she gave a shake of her head.

"What would ye have, lass?" He had to be sure.

"You," came the whispered answer. When had she ever wanted anything as much?

His breath rushed out in relief, and only then did

he realize he had been holding it. His hard length pressed against her soft belly. "Will you say my name then, Tess?"

"Aye," she imitated him, with a tiny quirk of a smile. She took a deep breath and sighed softly, "Ian."

"I've been awhile without the touch of a woman. But I still know how to be gentle. Ye needn't fear I'll hurt ye."

"And you?" she asked determinedly. If he could be so straightforward, so could she. "Are there ways, or places, I should not touch you?"

He tilted his head slightly and gave a tender half-smile. "I make ye free of this body, such as it is. There are scars, many of them, on more than my face. M'cheekbone is still sensitive. There was a lingerin' bit of infection. But if I cry out, lassie, I promise it will be in pure pleasure." That made her blush again, and the heat only deepened when he continued, "I've never known a grown woman to color so sweet." Then he smiled, and if she hadn't been lost before, she was now. "I've wanted ye since first I saw your hair spill from that rag Duke snatched off your head. You, Tess, with your eyes sad and soft as a sea mist."

Immeasurably touched, she looked at him. When she spoke, the voice didn't sound like her own. "Now I understand your far-reaching reputation with the females of the island, m'laird. You're nearly irresistible, aren't you?" Her smile was wry amusement that barely disguised how deeply his words affected her.

"Irresistible, no," he answered, and his expression revealed the bitterness he seldom let anyone see.

Tess felt as though her heart had dropped away. She'd hurt him. "There's more to a man than the side of his face, Ian. But I'm an artist. Maybe I'm peculiar."

For a long moment he looked into her eyes, over her face and down. "Ye're shaking," he said.

"So are you."

"Aye," he answered with a one-sided grin. "I am, as well."

"Ah . . ." She took a moment and let her gaze trace his features.

He held her naked hips in his hands, his fingers caressing her in little circling motions. But in the next instant Ian slipped her robe from her shoulders and let his hands glide down the sides of her torso. He gave a shudder of arousal that he could no longer suppress and inhaled sharply when he saw the vulnerable look in her eyes. He reached above his waist and dragged his thick sweater over his head. He wore an undershirt beneath, melded to the contours of his chest. A tuft of dark red hair showed above the seamed collar.

Tess couldn't resist pressing her palms to the rounded muscles visible beneath white cotton.

Warm. Strong. Compelling.

His hands moved to the center of her spine, sending lightning blazes of sensation through her abdo-

men to the place shivers came from. His heart beat
beneath her fingers, quickening at their movements.
Tess leaned forward to brush her nose back and forth
between her hands. She breathed deeply. First, crisp
cotton and soap. The heartbeat quickened even more.
He smelled of many things: the sea and long grasses,
man and sweat musk. There was even the faint scent
of leather. Her eyes closed, and her tongue darted out
to moisten lips that suddenly seemed dry.

She sighed in welcome of the pure pleasure of the
moment. Ian chuckled in answer.

"That's a nice sound," she told his undershirt,
her head still bent. Her palm pressed lightly. "Feels
good too."

"Mmm," he agreed with a low growl.

Her fingers curled slightly as they slid down over
his hard concave belly to his belt. After only a moment's
hesitation they drifted down his jeans to find the shape
of his arousal.

"Ah, God." Ian groaned into her hair, hardening
even more with her touch. His hand pressed her fingers tight against him. Another moan and his mouth
caught hers with a dark urgency she met immediately.
Her arms rose to his broad shoulders and tightened
until she could fit herself more perfectly to his hard
contours.

She'd never known such desire. It shuddered
through her, so strong it was a kind of pain. A
cry of both pleasure and frustration escaped from

her, only to be caught by Ian's deepening kiss as he pressed himself against her, brushing back and forth.

Her hands dragged the thin cotton of his undershirt upward until she made contact with bare skin. Her fingertips felt electrified as they traced muscle and ribs.

Ian kissed her swollen lips, her cheeks and eyes in languid motions. His mouth and tongue found the heartbeat at the base of her neck and shaped her collarbone, even as he cupped her breasts and sighed softly. He began a rhythmic massage.

When his mouth drew upon her nipple, Tess felt her knees weaken and the pulse throb between her legs.

"Aye," he whispered hotly against her white skin. His teeth worried the sensitive nub, and she cried out again.

His hands skimmed up her arms in one quick motion, drawing away to pull the undershirt over his head. He was a giant of a man, broad of chest and slim-waisted. Her eyes widened at the sight of the rich muscle on his arms and chest, the dark red pelt of hair. In the next instant Ian had grabbed her gently by the shoulders and pushed her back until she lay on the bed, knees bent over the side.

He dragged at the buttons on his jeans, shoved them down, and stepped away. When he straightened, his hot gaze painted her shape, and his arousal stood out from his body, dark and throbbing with each heartbeat.

Like his face, his left side was perfect, though the right leg was marked by far too many ugly scars from hip to ankle. Two were the straight lines of a scalpel from restorative operations, but most were burns. Still, his legs were long and very muscular, beautifully shaped. She wanted to run her hands over them.

"So you see." Ian's wary eyes never left hers. "I warned you there were scars."

Tess lifted her weight to her elbows and let her gaze slide over the magnificent body before her, taking in skin and muscle and bone and, yes, scars too. But to her those dark scars represented a moment when Ian chose to put everything on the line to save another. Every mark made him more attractive to her, a woman who was learning to love life again.

Sitting up, Tess reached for his hips and placed a slow, warm kiss upon the tip of his shaft, drawing a long groan from him. She had been celibate, but she was not inexperienced in what pleased a man. Smiling, she gave him an impudent lick before she trailed kisses down one side and up the other. She drew him into her mouth and let the sweet suction bring him to a gasping shiver. For a few moments more she pleasured him with her lips and teeth and tongue, treasuring every tortured sound he made. Finally, she pulled back to press kisses across his right hip, touching each scar she found.

They were still red and painful-looking, and they made her want to cry at what he had suffered, but she cherished every one of them. When she reached his knee, he dropped to the bed beside her.

"Ach, Tess. Come for me again." The deep green of his eyes glowed with tender heat as one hand slipped between her soft white thighs. He nuzzled her throat and whispered hoarsely, "Again, so I can feel it when I put m'self inside your honey heat." His long fingers moved tantalizingly over the hot, damp flesh, and she was soon convulsing around them.

He pressed her thighs apart, and in the next moment he was deep inside her, her muscles moving around him like molten velvet, tightening, caressing. He moaned in ecstasy and gave a shove of his hips, burying himself even farther within her. She was so tight, so burning hot!

His mouth found hers in a searing kiss, and she lunged upward, wanting him even more than she had before. Listening with her eyes closed, she reveled in the sounds of his harsh breathing. He began to move slowly, withdrawing until they were hardly joined before inching forward to fill her again. Each point of contact was electrifying; each tiny bit of friction sent her higher.

Shivering, moaning softly, she curled her long legs around his waist and clasped him tightly as his tongue dueled with hers. Faster and faster he moved, deeper than she thought possible. He rolled them over until she straddled him, pulled her legs from his waist, and watched her as he stroked her satiny thighs, then the backs of her knees, until he had coaxed her legs straight out on either side of him.

No green lad here, Tess thought in wonder, gasping. He smiled wickedly, sweat sliding down his temples.

It was the first time she had seen a real smile light his face, full and wide, without thought of how it might affect his appearance. His teeth flashed white.

It made her smile in return, and Ian wondered if he'd ever seen a more beautiful woman. She was flushed, and her dark silken hair clung damply to her neck and shoulders. Her eyes were blue pools of endless depth, and her tender, swollen mouth called for his kisses. His hands rose to her breasts, and he arched up until she sighed in wonder, "Oh, Ian! So . . . full, so deep!"

Her hands pressed his chest, sliding over his own sensitive nipples. Then she flexed her hips and gave a little sob, as if the sensations were simply too much. Helplessly, she moved again, and again, finding a rhythm that pleased them both until he groaned, closing her legs and rolling them over once more. This time he was at the edge of his control as he pushed her knees back, pumping in faster and faster motions until Tess sobbed her pleasure aloud. At the last Ian roared like a wild thing and shuddered as he gave himself to that sweet, fiery heaven.

Tess awoke in the night to find warm, comforting arms about her, and she was filled with such emotion she was frightened. Horribly frightened.

But what gifts he had given her, she thought, when he had given himself! He had made her feel cherished, so desired, when she had thought never to experience those things again. And she knew how difficult it must have been for him to open himself to her. He was too self-conscious of his face, his scars. Yet he had shared his vulnerability with her.

She had loved Ben deeply and abidingly, and their lovemaking had been a sweet extension of that caring. But never had she felt the wildness of the kind of passion Ian stirred in her. Such rare and exotic pleasure in the simplest touch. Wildfire.

It overwhelmed her.

Moving slowly, carefully, she raised her head from his shoulder and turned her face toward the hollow where his arm and body joined. She filled her lungs with the scent of him. Sweat and man—it was so erotic that she gave a little shiver, glancing up from under her lashes self-consciously. The brilliant green eyes studied her from his expressionless face, and she blushed, embarrassed. Her lips parted, although she had no notion of what she meant to say, and his mouth was suddenly hot upon hers as he let out a low, rumbling sound.

Pulling her body over his, Ian found his hardened shaft neatly caught between her legs. With a softly spoken "Ach," he pressed her thighs together with his hands, trapping his heat.

They clung together, sharing kiss after heated kiss, lips and tongues exploring, pleasuring, hands stroking. Tess flexed her hips, unable to keep them still. She wiggled until she felt his taut shaft press its heat where she needed it. He began biting at her lips and throat as her soft thighs tormented him with each shifting move.

"D'ye know how ye look to me?" he asked her hoarsely, brushing his rough, scarred cheek against her softness. "D'ye know how lovely?"

"Ian," she sighed his name, tears burning behind her eyelids. She was so grateful for these moments, for this man. She felt alive as she had not in two endless years, and that surging life made her feel reckless and happy.

With a strange quirk of a smile he acknowledged what he saw in her eyes: the hunger, the sweetness. In a quick reverse she was beneath him, facedown. He pulled her hands above her head and held them in one of his own. He stretched her arms upward to the brass headboard and curled her fingers to a firm grip. "Don't let go," he whispered as his tongue traced the shell-like whirls of that delicate cartilage, sending ripples of sensation to low in her spine, the center of her palms, even the sensitive arches of her feet. Grabbing a pillow, he pushed it under her belly to raise her hips to him.

He lifted the hair from her nape and, settling himself between her legs, let his arousal press against her thigh. Then he found her hairline with his mouth, nuzzling, biting, with tiny, delicious nibbles.

Lowering his body farther between the V of her thighs, Ian let both thumbs skim down her spine. It was as if he counted each vertebra, as though they were his to count. When he reached the perfect dimples above her rounded cheeks, he spent a good deal of time tracing them. He marked her sweet flesh with stinging little bites and soft kisses before he lightly traced the crevice between her buttocks. He explored downward until he found the warm place that swelled at his touch. . . .

FOUR

He hardly slept. The feel of her in his arms had kept him from it. That and thoughts of her.

Beauty. Secrets.

She had wanted, needed him. Her vulnerability was no facade.

But she was an American, here for an indefinite period of time, and he was scheduled to return to hospital tomorrow.

Morning came too soon. Tess had been lying awake in Ian's arms for nearly half an hour. Even as she savored every moment close to him, with the clear light of day, she forced herself to be realistic. In a moment of weakness she had given in to loneliness and physical desire.

The entire week she'd been home, he'd occupied

her thoughts. He was really quite a gentle man, and kind. But since she had returned, she had listened more closely to the stories told by the locals. Ian MacLeod was one of Britain's darlings, an intimate of the royals who spent much of the year abroad, playing polo, sailing, fishing for salmon, and enjoying other pursuits of the wealthy aristocracy. It was difficult to imagine Ian's gruff manners charming the rich and famous. That, more than anything, made her realize this time was just an unfortunate interlude for the laird MacLeod.

"Tess?" Looking down, he could see the blink of her long eyelashes.

"Mm," she answered, somehow making no commitment with the sound.

"It's after nine, lass, past time for me to go."

"Go?" she whispered carefully.

"Aye, I've a train to catch to Edinburgh." He brushed her hair back from her face, admiring her widow's peak, the silky texture of the strands that caught between his fingers. "And surgery tomorrow."

"Ian?" She lifted herself above him and looked down. "How dangerous?"

"Not a bit," he answered, covering the effect her concern had upon him. " 'Tis only reconstructive."

"Oh," she said thoughtfully, pulling the sheet up with her as she sat back against the pillows. An easy out for both of them then.

"It's rather a long process, six or eight weeks," he

continued carefully. The stillness of her expressive face bothered him. "But I'd like to see more of you when I get back."

What a nice, practiced phrase, Tess thought as she turned and looked to the window and out across the meadow—anywhere but at him.

She, the shy, eccentric American artist, he, the European playboy backed by centuries of wealth and tradition. A femme fatale she had never been; neither was he the country squire. And now he, quite naturally, would assume that she was ready to become one of the women who chased him for a chance to share in the glamour. He'd have his surgery, be back to form and ready to take up his old life. But they had had one unforgettable night, and she would treasure the memory.

"Oh . . ."—she smoothed a bit of the coverlet—"I expect we'll both be pretty busy." She concentrated on stilling the tremor in her voice. "And to tell you the truth, I don't even know if I'll be here in two months."

Ian couldn't have been more stunned if she had hit him with a block of wood. His chest wanted to cave in with the surprise of it as he stared at her profile. Hadn't she felt it? Had he been the only one? How could that be?

He flushed with embarrassment and stifled a rough laugh. He supposed it served him right. He had taken women casually, even Fiona, thinking that the laughter and physical pleasure, the companionship, were enough. In truth he had thought that was all there was. Now, when he had finally made a connection to a woman that was so strong, so completely *right*, he wondered if their very thoughts had joined, she dealt with him as he had dealt with too many others.

He had to get out of there *now*, he thought, scanning the room to locate his clothes. "Well, then," he kept his voice casual, "Ranald will still be across the way if ye've need of him." He yanked up one leg of his pants, then the other. "He'll feed Duke." Shirt, boots, his motions were mechanical. "Do have a care where ye walk."

Tess was holding back tears with desperate determination when she felt the give of the mattress and realized he sat right in front of her. Her gaze went to the top of his unbuttoned shirt. She couldn't speak, but the words ran round and round inside her mind: *Tell me it was different for you, that it was important, that I'm important, and you won't let me go!*

Stop me! Ian's heart cried. But she wouldn't even look at him. He took a long breath and hardened his jaw. So be it.

He snatched her to him, enveloping her in his strong arms, overwhelming her. His eyes found hers with a frightening intensity. Then he ravished her mouth with his tongue until, at last, she murmured her desire against his lips, and her hand rose to his rough cheek in a shaky caress. That was what he had waited for, what his pride needed.

"Thanks, little Yank. T'was one hell of a night!" With that he left her, pounding down the steps, slamming the door behind him.

For the first two weeks Tess told herself things had turned out for the best. She certainly wasn't cut out to be a playboy's mistress. And if she became a little weepy in the evenings, she told herself it was just that her emotions had been dead for so long, they had to adjust. Still, she relived the hours she had spent with Ian over and over again. She even found herself watching for him, as if he might magically appear around a corner or through the mist.

She wondered about the outcome of the operation, although Ian had told her there was no danger. She hadn't heard any talk about it and wished she had the courage to ask someone the name of the hospital, but Ian had told her how he felt about gossip. So she tried to content herself with whatever she might hear by chance.

A week after he left, Ranald came to get Duke for his supper, and Tess found she couldn't wait any longer.

"Can I get you a cup of tea, Ranald?" she offered. Her nervousness made him give a quick nod of agreement.

"Is there something wrong, miss?" he finally asked after swallowing a bite of raisin scone.

"I was just, um, wondering how the laird's operation went?"

Ranald was no fool. He saw in her face that the American lass had more than a casual interest. He had thought the laird had been rather interested in her as well.

"Och, the lad came through the first of them fine enough. But there'll be a whole series to get through in the next couple of months." Ranald took a sip of tea and watched her. Here it comes, he thought.

"I wonder," Tess began, "if I could ask you a favor?"

"Of course, miss."

Her hands twisted in her lap, but she forced herself to go on. "I'd like it to be confidential."

He could see how difficult this was for her and took pity. "Anything I can do, miss, and it will be just between us." Then he watched the color come to her lovely face.

"Thank you, Ranald. You're very kind." She took a deep breath. "It's only . . . I'd like to know how he's doing—the laird, I mean. But I don't want to make a fuss or . . . have people talking."

"It would be no trouble at all, miss," Ranald answered, glad that it was something within his power to perform. "And I willna breath a word, except to himself."

"Oh, no!" Her cup rattled against the saucer. "Not to anyone!"

Ranald studied her again. He supposed she had her reasons. "Whatever you say, miss."

She felt much better after that. Ranald would keep his word.

And when Tess made her first real attempt to paint again, it was the great man's portrait she painted.

It started with the series of sketches she made from the hill that overlooked the loch. No matter what she began with, his image was so clear in her mind that she wound up with study after study of his face and form against those landscapes.

Finally, one sleepless night, she stood before a blank canvas and began. And when she started, there was no stopping.

With her return to painting, a sense of well-being warmed her life. Tess began to bloom. She listened to the women who came to Janet's store complaining of their need for day care, winter industry, and life for the men away from the pubs. So many of the men had to leave the Isle out of season, some never to return, others changed.

Those who remained depended on savings or odd jobs, while the women sewed or used their looms to make some money to see them through. Some dug the small black snails the French craved called "winkies" or "wilks," though no Islander would be caught eating them. But that was backbreaking work, digging the shore for hours, then dragging their harvest half a mile uphill to the road.

Tess sketched their faces, paying a small sitting fee, and she listened to their stories, their troubles.

And, because she was an irrepressible American after all, she began talking about an idea Janet's weaving had given her some time ago. In the weeks that followed she set up a system for export of island crafts to New York through Janet's store, getting the help of an old friend in the States. It was a small business, but it benefited anyone who cared to have a hobby exported. Within weeks it made Tess something of a local heroine, especially when she arranged to turn a percentage of the profits back to the fund for the day care/community center. No business was sacred there, and Janet and Elsbeth saw to it with loving energy.

Over the next weeks Tess enlisted Ranald's aid, and they poked around until they found that the largest building in town, a vacant hotel some Englishman had abandoned, could be leased for next to nothing. It needed only a few repairs the men would have no trouble completing. There was a pool table and a wide lawn for either shinty or football.

Geordie volunteered to teach carving to any who wanted to learn, and Ranald said he would teach boys and girls how to train their young sheepdogs. Janet and Elsbeth organized a committee to take turns with the refreshments, and Betty Doon gave gourmet cooking lessons. A joyous contagion overcame the village.

Tess had only to mention new programs being set up in the States that combined day care for the aged with that of toddlers, with benefits to both, and the idea was eagerly seized upon. When she borrowed Ranald's crop of kittens and puppies and took them to the center to encourage the generations to communicate, Elsbeth cried to see the joy on her mother's aged face as she cradled a four-year-old in her arms and instructed her in the way to hold a puppy for the very first time.

"But she's no' spoken a word since Da's death ten months past!" Elsbeth whispered in awe, dabbing at her eyes with her apron. Janet nodded and gave Tess's hand a squeeze.

From that day Tess found herself truly part of their world, for Janet and Elsbeth had decided to take her personally in hand.

They watched her schedule and conferred. Seven A.M. to noon she painted. By one o'clock she had made her way down to the community center, where she flattered, cajoled, and bargained with Islanders to pose. Before the fireplace, Duke at her feet, she sketched to her heart's content. And so her own art classes began.

Evenings she garnered so many dinner invitations, she had to turn down half a dozen for each night of the week. Janet had long since wormed every bit of her past out of her, excluding her time with Ian, and Tess was quite sure that half the matchmakers on the Isle had made her their target. Elsbeth had the responsibility of dressing her. She had the sewing class making their samples to her exact measurements, forcing Tess to suffer through endless fittings. Finally, Tess had to insist on supplying materials, and of course she had to wear their efforts, for the sake of their pride.

She took the stitches out of Ben's pants and packed away the rest of his things before she finally gave them to the kirk.

Her life was full, though she still thought about Ian much too often. Then one day when Elsbeth was fitting her for a red velvet sheath, the older woman's round face creased and plumped as she smoothed and adjusted the soft material over Tess's stomach. Her motions slowed, and she looked up at Tess and blinked in her meaningful way.

"What is it, El?" Tess asked. The older woman had a look on her face Tess had never seen before.

"I'm thinkin' we'll have to put larger seams in these dresses, dear."

"What?" Tess asked, puzzled.

Elsbeth stood then and took her arm, leading her to the kitchen. There, she blinked her brown eyes again and pushed Tess into a chair. Plumping herself down at the table, she reached for Tess's hand, holding it tightly between both of her own soft, dark-spotted ones as she said, "Did ye no' ken?" She rubbed her thumb over Tess's knuckles. Bewildered silence followed, then she sighed deeply. " 'Tis my belief ye carry a bairn, lassie."

Tess felt her vision blur for a dizzy moment, and she shook her head, drawing a deep breath. Suddenly, a warm smile blossomed and grew. Her free hand slipped to her newly rounded abdomen under the covered buttons.

"Do you really think so, El?" she whispered in a frightened kind of wonder. "I knew I was gaining a bit of weight. But I'm so hungry all the time, and . . . sleepy. Do you really think . . . ?" Happiness radiated from her like a light as she looked at the hands that covered hers. "Could it be?"

Elsbeth was pleased to see the happiness on Tess's face as she answered with a last soft sweep of her fingertips over Tess's taut belly. "And am I no' the midwife o' Dunvegan?"

Tess felt her face crumble, and she hugged the plump white-haired woman to her. "Thank you, Elsbeth," she sighed. "You can't know what . . . thank you!" she whispered.

She couldn't get dressed in her own clothes quickly enough, and she traversed the mile home without ever even realizing that Elsbeth had sent Ranald after her to make sure she got there all right.

Still in a daze, she called Dr. MacInnes's office in Portree for an appointment the next day.

In the morning Elsbeth appeared at her door with her abbreviated station wagon as if by magic. Pushing aside the front-window curtain, Tess gave a wry smile and wondered if news of her condition was all over the island. This would certainly be an interesting addition to the story of the Yank on the hill.

Bundling against the chill morning winds, Tess locked up and got into the wagon as if it had been prearranged.

"There now," Elsbeth clucked as Tess buckled her seat belt. "We're all set. I'll drive slow; we've plenty of time."

Tess couldn't think of anything Elsbeth resembled more than a Disney fairy godmother. In fact, both Janet and Elsbeth fit those childhood memories.

Bibitty-bobitty-boo!

She had no idea why the idea made her feel so safe. "So you're in cahoots with the doctor," Tess accused lightly, wondering what bribe Elsbeth had used to make Janet stay out of this little episode.

"Och, Hamish is m'godson, don't you know. An' a grand doctor he is. It so happened that I called to make ye an appointment, and I found ye had already made the arrangements."

"I . . . would like . . . to keep this confidential, Elsbeth." Tess looked away.

"Well, now." Elsbeth cleared her throat and looked into a far corner. "We all look out for each other here on the Isle, lass. . . ."

"You mean you've told Janet already?"

"Ye didna ask me to keep it a secret. An' ye'll only find friends here for ye as ye need them. Ye've brought so verra much to us," Elsbeth sputtered in her own defense. She gave Tess a shrewd look and sighed, before she countered, "Have ye contacted the father, lass?"

"The bog's getting a bit thick under your feet as it is, don't you think, Elsbeth?" Tess warned, and the other woman sighed, then concentrated on her driving.

Elsbeth lifted her chins and smiled to herself. She'd simply have to have a word with dear Angus. He was quite fond of her meat pie, she remembered.

FIVE

The laird had returned.

Both the store and the center had been buzzing with the news. Elsbeth, excited by what Angus had told her, had already made it a point to drop by the dower house at teatime to invite the laird to Friday night's opening *ceilidh*. She went on about the center and how Tess was its driving force, about the changes it had made in the community.

Ian listened, trying to keep his interest from being too apparent, but he drank in every word. And when she left, he drank Ranald's home brew, trying to drive thoughts of the lass across the road from his mind.

Friday came. Tess knew Janet and Elsbeth suspected Ian was the father of her baby when they both appeared at her house that evening to help her dress and give her a ride. They managed to slip it into the conversation that himself had returned, beautifully, surgically healed. When they began stories of the amusing pranks of his childhood, she was certain.

Tess was deliberately casual, wondering if she was going to be the evening's entertainment. She didn't see the looks that passed between her two fairy god-mothers.

He stepped into the ballroom and stood in the wide doorway, taking in the scents of lemon and bees-wax, aged wood and leather, women's perfume. It was a grand room, with dark wood and mirrors about. A band played on a stage that stood at one end, and the floor was crowded with dancers.

Ian took a great breath and squared his shoulders. This would be his first confrontation with his peo-ple. The idea made his blood run cold. Then he saw young Meggie waving to him from the arms of her smiling mother and heard the first notes as the pipes began to play his clan song. He looked to the stage, and there stood Angus, cheeks puffed out as he played, eyes twinkling. The music echoed through Ian's head and gave him strength.

He turned left, then right. The room was full of people he'd known all his life, people he had avoided for the last months. They looked at him with accept-ance, with affection. A pounding started in his chest, and he realized that it had always been there, but he had not had the eyes to see.

Tess felt her heart gladden at the sight of him. The soft glow of the aged lamps placed around the room flattered his sharp profile. He wore a buff-colored suede jacket over a pale sweater. A hush fell. Suddenly, she realized why.

Gone was her rough, embittered Heathcliff. In his place was the man who belonged to the British aristocracy, arrogant and devastatingly handsome. Their laird stood tall, at ease, looking all comers eye-to-eye. His scars were now almost completely unnoticeable, pale against his jaw. The emerald eyes sparkled with amusement, and the wild mane of auburn hair shifted around his shoulders, emphasizing their width.

Here was the bold charmer, the lady-killer whose exploits were the delight of British press and British pubs. And Tess felt her smile of welcome falter, for she didn't know him at all.

He saw her far across the room. He didn't think she'd seen him yet. She looked glorious—but different somehow. It might have been the dress she wore, or the fact that she wore a dress. She was radiant, and he knew a deep need to get to her side.

Elsbeth chose that moment to step up to the stage. She bobbed along to the microphone and leaned forward. "May I . . . ahem! . . . may I have yer attention, ladies and gentlemen, please!" When the noise didn't die down fast enough for her, the plump little woman cleared her throat noisily, then finally tapped her finger against the mike. Boom-boom, boom-boom. "Good evening, ladies and gentlemen. Welcome to the Dunvegan Community Center. We're here to celebrate the opening of the center . . . and to thank our founder, a most welcome addition to our community, Miss Tess Hartley. She has brought new life and grand ideas to the Isle, and for that we thank her." Then Elsbeth began the applause that nearly lifted the roof.

Tess blushed and smiled and looked around helplessly. Moments passed, and Ian finally gave a subtle hand signal to Angus. The small band of musicians broke into a well-known folk tune. He walked across the room, and then he simply held out his arms to her. Once again, Tess flushed and looked around self-consciously. She realized the honor he was doing her in front of the villagers as she stepped into his arms. They danced for long minutes without words.

"Ye're a fine sight, lass," Ian bent and murmured at last for her ears alone. "I was afraid ye might be back in the States by now." When she didn't answer, he said, "Ye've made quite a few changes in m'wee village. This center . . . I've heard about yer day care and craft business, as well. Ye've brought Yankee prosperity here, Tess."

"You've been gone a long time," she answered without expression, though her heart was pounding in her breast and her cheeks were afire. She wondered if he minded all the changes—his "m'wee village" remark sounded pretty possessive.

"Aye. 'Tis glad I am ye're still here. I would have had to track ye down. . . ."

Tess pulled away with a jerk as the song finished. "Please, Ian. You don't owe me any explanations."

Ian scowled and started to speak, but she shook her head, "No, I'm serious." She looked serene and so bonnie with her sea-blue eyes and the dark silk of her hair. "We were both lonely. What happened, happened." Then she looked up at him and smiled, and he could think of nothing save how beautiful she was. "You don't know what you gave me that night. And I'll never be able to repay you."

Ian looked embarrassed, a flush slipping up from his own strong neck to cheeks. He assumed she was talking about getting over her grief. He didn't like thinking about that.

Tess flushed in response, careful of revealing too much. "I'm painting again, and I never thought I would." She smiled sadly and looked him right in the eyes. "I'm glad your face has healed so well. I know it was important to you."

Ian had no intention of leaving things at that, but young Jaimie Blair stood before them and, in an instant, had taken Tess into his arms and swung her away. Ian felt a touch on his arm and caught the scent of peppermint as he looked around to find Angus standing before him.

"I'd have a word with ye, m'laird," he stated quietly.

"Aye, Angus." Ian was startled. A child of the Isle, he would never ignore a summons from Angus MacCrimmon, piper to the clan as the MacCrimmons had been from ancient times.

Angus drew him toward the cloakroom and sent the lass who was tending it to find refreshments.

"Ian, lad," Angus started, his lined face full of secrets. Ian looked down at him, knowing that the secrets were for him.

"Aye. What is it, Angus?" he asked warily, knowing the old man's power.

"Ye're m'laird, an' ye've all my loyalty," he began. "The clan has stood strong for hundreds o' years, and has always been behind my own in times o' trouble." He gave Ian a hard look. " 'Tis clan business that brings me. First, about the fire that destroyed MacGregor's croft and near took the lives of his family and yerself."

Ian straightened grimly. "Has there been more trouble then?"

" 'Tis what I expect. Though the eve of the MacGregor fire, the family was thought to be in Glasgow with Lucy's parents."

"D'ye ken why they stayed?" Ian looked hard into the deep gray eyes.

"The bairn had a fever."

"Did ye 'see' it, old friend?" Ian asked quietly.

"Nay," Angus shook his head slowly as he answered, "though I wish I had. I'd know the devil then."

"But why such a wanton act of destruction?" Ian demanded, "What is this about, Angus?"

" 'Tis the bridge, Ian, and the money it will bring to the Isle. MacGregor's been for it, loud and long. The owners of pubs like his and the town merchants know the extra pounds it'll bring. But the landowners, the crofters, and the conservationists dinna want the land more disturbed by added tourists. I've heard a tale that there are even outside interests trying to buy property in Portree for a grand hotel. People are fearful of change, lad. The last of the council meetings are close upon us, and I fear for the violence."

"Do not worry, cousin." Ian put one hand upon the old man's shoulder. "We'll spread a quiet word and see if we can ferret out these troublemakers. But come to me straight away d'ye have more information. 'Tis a miracle the MacGregor child wasna burned to death. We want no riots on the Isle." Angus nodded, but when Ian turned back to the door, Angus stopped him, a strange light in his eyes.

"There's more, laddie." There was something in Angus's voice that sent a chill through Ian, and his brow darkened with concern. "I'll no hold back that which ye've a right to know." He waited a moment, as if it were a decision he was reluctant to make. Ian's senses sharpened as he waited. Finally, Angus announced, "The American lassie carries yer heir."

Angus let that sink in for a moment, seeing the confusion, then the slow joy, before he went on, "An' if ye don't take care, you may lose the both of them."

That was when Fiona came through the door with her canny feline smile and pulled Ian back into the hall as she chattered at him. Stunned, Ian followed her, though he was barely aware of the woman or the music.

Oh, Fiona was a beauty, from her soft white-blond hair to her long, sleek legs. And Ian saw now the small-spirited woman she had become. But he hadn't seen through the haze of his sexual infatuation until he was in the hospital right after the fire and still in shock, crazy with the pain.

Fiona had pasted a stiff smile upon her face when she first came into the room. But when she saw the extent of his injuries, she had recoiled in horror. Until then, he hadn't given a thought to the change in his appearance.

But that was a moment he would never forget. She couldn't even bring herself to touch his hand. Her words to him were sweet, but tainted with her obvious revulsion.

When she left, he had choked back tears of humiliation and thought over all the time they had shared. At last, near the end of that sleepless night, he came to see her for the shallow, pleasure-seeking, manipulative woman she was. He remembered, too, her fondness for his money.

Strange, he reflected, how those thoughts now prevented the weight of her firm breasts against his arm from affecting him in a sexual way. Aye, strange indeed, when he had only to look across the room at the black silk of Tess's hair shining down her back in the yellow lamplight to be instantly aroused.

"Dance with me, Ian," Fiona demanded prettily. When she saw his hesitation, she flashed her great brown eyes and went on, "Or they'll call me 'poor Fiona' and whisper how ye jilted me from your hospital bed." Then she watched his eyes dart to the American girl in the red velvet dress. "Only one dance, Ian," she finished, holding back her rancor with a tight rein.

Ian gave a short sigh and took her in his arms because he knew Fiona was right, and more gossip would truly hurt her. But when they were only halfway round a turn, she said the unforgivable: "You look wonderful. The scars are almost—"

"Nay," he interrupted harshly, "they're still there, every great ugly one of them."

"Now, Ian . . ." Fiona tightened her lips and saw him glance again at the dark-haired girl. Her chin lifted, and she spit out nastily, "She's knocked up, ye know."

Ian's arms tightened painfully around her. "What did ye say?"

Fiona smirked in satisfaction. "The American. Pregnant, and quite single, I hear. Then why else come to the Isle in winter? I imagine she's trying to hide her little bastard away here. But she'll go back to the States soon. They all do." And all the while Fiona droned on about how loud and rude Americans were, Ian kept his glazed eyes focused straight ahead.

Common gossip! But why hadn't Tess told him? Just what did she intend?

Tess was kept quite busy, either on the dance floor or in the kitchen. Although Ian felt his mind racing, he wasn't ready to speak to her. He kept thinking about her last words to him and the way she looked in that red dress . . . and how the scent of her had stayed with him.

He thought about the feel of her against him when they were dancing. The lush softness of her breasts and the press of her hard little belly against him. *He had a bairn of his own coming! An' what would sweet Aileen say to that?*

He saw Tess dancing with Douglas Firth and found he didn't care for how close the fisherman held her or the smile she gave him at the turn. Ian tossed back a whisky as he saw Colin MacDonald take her into the next reel. For the rest of the night he watched Tess, waiting for her to come to him, to tell him they needed to talk . . . anything. But she wouldn't so much as look at him, even when he danced past her with pretty Kitty Firth in his arms.

There did come, however, a moment when Angus cornered her in the kitchen.

" 'Tis glad I am to see ye bloom so among us, lassie," he said, helping himself to a thick sandwich, taking in the red dress and her woman's curves.

"Thank you, Angus," Tess told him, pouring a glass of mineral water. "You were my very first friend on the Isle. I've never heard the pipes live before. It's a wonderful noise." She grinned and let the grin widen as Angus gave her a courtly bow.

Then he twinkled at her and passed her a quarter-section of his sandwich. Tess smiled in appreciation and took a bite. That's when, all sweet innocence and gentle concern, he said, "Aye, ye'll want to build yer strength. The male heirs of the MacLeods are born the size o' giants." Tess choked until the old man pounded between her shoulders.

"Why would you . . . how, um . . . excuse me." Then she blushed and backed away, pushing the swinging door with her hips, whirling around to race to the cloakroom.

She was going to murder Elsbeth!

It was late when she slipped out alone. Ian knew she intended to walk home. He had other plans.

Fiona watched Ian follow the dark-haired Yank and burned.

Driving up the black tar road, Ian found her some two hundred feet from the village. She whirled around at the sudden glare of headlights and recognized the driver before she drew her collar high and pointed her flashlight homeward once again. He pulled up with a screech of brakes and lowered the window near her.

"What d'ye think ye're doing out here on yer own this time of night?" he demanded angrily.

"I'm going home," Tess returned in an irritated tone of voice. Entirely too many people were taking a personal interest in her life these days.

"An' anyone who wishes could attack you!"

She turned back toward her destination. "That's ridiculous."

"Get into the car, Tess," he said in a slow, deliberate rumble, "before I put ye in it m'self!"

She stared at him a moment, wondering how he dared. Then she finally gave in, thinking wryly that this man would dare anything. They drove the rest of the short mile in silence. When he pulled up in front of her cottage, he got out and strode around the car to help her out with an air of purpose. At the front door he followed her inside, putting one hand in the middle of her back to give her a gentle push forward, into the living room. There, he took her coat and his own to hang them near the door.

When he returned, Tess thought of the first time he'd forced his way into the cottage as she asked in perfect, artificial welcome, "Would you care for tea?"

Ian turned toward her, his dark thick lashes half-lowered. "There's talk about the village." He spoke in a strained monotone she'd never before heard from him. His hot glance swept over her, searching for changes. He looked deep into her blue eyes and saw the confirmation there. "I've come to see for m'self," he told her, his voice low and gruff. As he stepped impossibly close to her, Tess was stunned when he reached for the first of the red velvet buttons that ran down the front of her dress. He undid them, one after the other, with slow, deliberate motions, and knelt before her.

Her breath quickened, and her heart began to pound. She could no more have stopped him than she could have stopped breathing.

His eyes caressed the new fullness of her breasts that he uncovered. They nearly spilled from the sheer black lace, nipples hardening beneath his gaze. He had heard that a woman's breasts were extraordinarily sensitive during pregnancy.

The back of his knuckles brushed over the silky skin that overflowed, and he watched her eyes dilate. His own were steady and purposeful. Glancing lower, her waist seemed even smaller, her ribs visible. Then he saw the slight protrusion of her stomach and placed the heat of his palm there, pressing lightly against the firm swell.

"You said . . . what I gave you, you could never repay," he whispered, and when his eyes met hers, unbidden tears slipped down her cheeks.

"Yes." She expelled a long breath.

"Mine." He sighed softly.

Looking down at him, she blinked quickly as she wondered if he questioned that.

"Yes," she responded, while the feel of his hand upon her stomach made her want to cry out. Heat raced in her veins, settling between her thighs with a burning ache.

Ian stared at her slight belly for some time before he got slowly to his feet and buttoned her buttons.

"I should have protected you." He stepped away to the window and glared into the darkness.

"It was as much my responsibility as yours," she answered, annoyed at his attitude.

He whirled back to her and demanded harshly, "Was it deliberate then?"

She looked at him a long time. There was no reproach in her eyes for the accusation, only a deep sincerity. "No, Ian. But I'm not sorry it happened either."

Then he shocked her. He smiled. A sweet, delighted, possessive kind of smile that made her want to smile back.

"So, ye'll . . . wish to marry, lass," Ian said lightly, turning once again to the window. "I can call for the special license in the morning."

"What?" Tess froze; she could hardly believe her ears.

"Even if you dinna wish to stay married," the laird announced, turning back to her and stepping close enough to look down into her face. "We owe it to the bairn to give it a name."

Tess faced Ian, pushing her hair back over her shoulder in a determined swipe. "My child will have a name. My name." He flushed and opened his mouth, but she spoke before he had a chance. "There's no shotgun here, Ian, for either of us."

He took a moment to consider his words before he spoke, trying to stay reasonable and still his own panic. Would she run from him to the States? "Were ye even planning to tell me?" he asked gruffly.

"Of course," she answered, shocked at the question. She looked down. "I just might have . . . taken more time to do it."

Even in the midst of this, Ian was captivated. He placed his warm hand against her cheek. " 'Tis my bairn as well."

Her chin lifted, and she stared intently into his green eyes. "And you will always have full visitation rights, Ian. I would never deny you that. It wouldn't be fair to you or the baby. But marriage . . . Ian, we hardly know each other. You don't know me. You don't know me at all. I paint for hours, with no care for the time passing. I'm shy . . . and I'd rather putter in a garden than go shopping in designer stores. Polo bores me to tears." When it looked as though he might interrupt with an objection, she raced on. "I like to have my own way, and my politics are strictly liberal. I'd argue with all your friends, and you'd tire of me in a matter of weeks." Even as she said the words, her heart protested. She couldn't look at the possibility of marriage to this man. He was the laird of the MacLeods, darling of the Isle, and she didn't want a cover-up marriage, even for their baby. She felt a shiver run up her spine. Her baby would be forever connected to this Isle and the MacLeod family.

He let her have her say, shoulders wide and stiff, but he still had to ask, "Ye won't leave that to me then?"

"Let's talk about names instead." Tess couldn't focus.

"An' ye'll no' disappear to the States?" Ian demanded abruptly.

"What about the press, the gossip?"

He frowned down at her. "D'ye think me so small that I would deny my own bairn for gossip or gutter press?"

Tess reached for his big hand and let hers curl around it. "No, Ian." She sighed. "And I'll stay. I promise you." She looked into his eyes. "Until the baby is born. We'll decide what will be best for all of us after that." Then she released his hand because she wanted to hold on to it so badly. "But you have to know something. I feel no shame about this baby, only joy, and I won't let you or anyone else make me regret the miracle of this child."

He didn't understand the liquid warmth that ran through him at her words. He looked again over her tiny waist and the flow of her hips and imagined the way she was going to look in the months to come as she swelled with his child. "Fair enough," he said at last, not certain what else to say. His problem now was how to convince her to share those precious moments with him. He was suddenly worried. "Do you feel all right?"

Tess nodded with a wide, beautiful smile. "I'm . . . due in early June, Ian."

He stared down at her and finally said, with absolutely no expression, "It's lovely here in June. The weather's warm and gentle, and the air smells sweeter than anywhere on earth." Sighing, he ran one hand through his wine-dark mane of hair and turned to leave. "Well, then . . ." He needed to think. There was so much to think about. "I'll leave you to your rest for now. But I'll come by tomorrow." His hand rose, as if he might have brushed her cheek, but he faltered and said a simple "Good night."

Trembling from the simple effect of his nearness, Tess unclenched her hands and swallowed her disappointment at the sound of the front door closing behind him.

SIX

He was on her doorstep at noon the next day with his housekeeper and something in a big, crinkled brown paper bag.

"This is Callie." Ian turned to the tall, gaunt, middle-aged woman whose expression looked as though she sucked lemons and sipped vinegar. "And this is Ms. Hartley."

" 'Tis pleased I am to meet ye, miss. Though I've seen ye about the village." The woman bobbed her head and tried to smile, which made Tess realize that Callie couldn't do anything about her expression. It was a natural, frozen grimace.

Bewildered, Tess nodded and stood aside to let them into the cottage. Callie bobbed her head again and made a beeline for the kitchen. Tess's arm reached straight out after her, and she stared in amazement before turning back to Ian. "Where is she . . . what is she doing?"

"What she does best, taking charge," he answered, looking after the bustling figure with great fondness as he stepped into the hall.

"What are you talking about?" Tess wondered.

"Yer health, and that of our child. Callie will take care o' ye both."

"What do you mean, take care?" She turned back to him, her anger lying beneath the surface but still quite evident.

"Whate'er ye need. Ye can let Callie know." Ian met her eyes.

"So I'm a puppy you farm out?" she demanded, with more sheer fury than she remembered ever feeling. "Is that what you're saying? Or maybe you're telling me that you're providing for me now?"

"An' if I am?" he asked, bending down to her, his proud face before hers. "Is it not my bairn you carry?"

"I'll have you know, Laird MacLeod, that I am quite capable of providing for this child—"

"Our child!" he inserted indignantly.

"Our child." She caught herself, took a calming breath, and amended in an amazingly reasonable tone, "You have every right to be concerned about the baby, Ian. But *after* it's born, don't you think? I can take care of things myself now."

"Not if ye listen to what they're saying in the

village," he started in a frustrated voice. He certainly looked angry. His stance was sturdy and sure. "They say ye work too long and far too hard! Both here and at your center. Up, painting two hours before the light, then organizing and teaching and such until long after dark. But ye've more to think of than just yourself now."

"You have spies on me?" She whirled around on him, incensed. "You dare?"

"Why would I need spies? 'Tis common gossip." He scowled. Then his face softened as he said, "Ye're not alone in this, lass. With all yer work, the house and the cooking could be too much for any one person." When he saw that Tess was about to argue, he went on, "Please, Tess, I'm asking you to let me have a place in this part of our bairn's life, to let me help."

The man had a talent for getting his own way, but when he put it like that, she simply melted—anger, bones, and any vestige of sense.

She looked down and changed the subject to draw attention away from her easy defeat. "What's in the bag?"

Silence followed until she finally looked back up at him. Why, the great man was blushing! Now this was interesting!

He held the sack out to her with a stiff elbow, and she took it from him with a certain wariness. The paper crackled loudly in her ears as she spread the top open. Ian wondered if he would ever forget the expression on her face as she pulled the ancient hand-stitched brown teddy bear from the bag.

"Yours?" She stared at it in wonder. When he didn't answer, she glanced up to see him looking rueful. At last he nodded his head. She would never have expected such sentiment from him. "It's in wonderful condition."

"M'mother repaired it once or twice, I believe," he said enigmatically. "And that brings me to something I've a need to speak to ye about." His feet shuffled a bit; he pulled at one ear and pleaded, "D'ye think we could go into the parlor, lass?"

"Of course, Ian," she answered, thinking she'd never seen him like this. He looked like a small boy who had decided for the first time that he liked a girl. He was so uncomfortable.

When they sat next to each other on the couch, he rubbed his big hands together gingerly before he said, "I had to go to the castle nursery to retrieve . . . um . . . the bear."

"Yes . . ." she coaxed.

"I'm afraid my . . . mother caught me there."

Tess grinned gleefully. Here was another side she'd not seen before. "You're afraid of your mother?" She had to smother a giggle.

A haughty red brow raised, and dignity gathered close. "No! I mean, well, no! However . . ." He paused meaningfully before he announced, "I have been asked to deliver an invitation to tea."

"How nice." Tess gave a tentative smile back and said, "I wasn't aware your mother was on the island. She probably wants to discuss the center."

Ian stood up quickly and made his way to the barstand against one wall. "May I?" he asked her over his shoulder. When she nodded, he helped himself to a shot of whisky. Then he took a deep breath and turned around to face her. "The lady Aileen resides in Edinburgh or parts south in the winter. It was a surprise that she returned—and it is specifically because she wishes to meet you, lass."

Tess was stunned and stammered out, "Elsbeth's gossip has reached as far as Edinburgh?"

Ian gave a knowing grin. "Ye can never be certain where a Scot obtains information, lass. But she's made it quite clear that she expects us both on Sunday."

"For an inquisition?" Tess sat up straight. "I think not."

Ian hardly knew what to say to that. "If ye refuse her invitation, Tess, she'll simply descend upon you here. Couldn't we just go have a friendly cup of tea and satisfy her curiosity?"

Tess stood up and moved to the fireplace, still clutching the homely teddy bear. "What a thought. Yes, I'm sure I'll enjoy being a curiosity."

"Now, Tess," he said calmingly. Somehow he was right behind her, placing his hands upon her shoulders. "Aileen's no dragon, I can promise ye. She's simply a middle-aged mother who's learned she's soon to be a grandmother. She's excited."

"Hmmph!" Tess didn't believe it. "Even *you're* afraid of her."

Callie chose that moment to appear in the doorway.

"I've m'list, now, sir. And if the lady will tell me what time she wishes dinner?"

"It's Tess, Callie," Tess interrupted.

Ian smiled to himself, thinking his Yank would never change Callie or her sense of what was proper.

But Tess went on, "And thank you, but I'll just throw together a salad tonight." She sighed as Callie looked most disapproving. Then she tried a smile. "Tomorrow will be soon enough for all these lovely changes."

"As ye wish, Miss Tess." Callie bobbed her head, "M'laird. I'll be getting along then."

"Ye'll allow me to escort ye to tea at the castle then?" Ian asked.

"Sunday?" Tess swallowed hard, thinking she'd have to ask Elsbeth what to wear. Ian inclined his head. "All right." Then her head shot up. "But I'm warning you now, Ian, if she says anything disparaging about this baby . . ."

"Don't fret, love," he reassured her quickly, "that would never happen. First, the lady has no prejudice. Second, the lady is a lady. And, if by wildest chance, she were to make such a comment, I would leave with ye."

The endearment had shocked her so much that she heard the rest only in echo. But when the words finally sank in, she turned a shy smile on him.

It hit him like a fist in the gut, and he was quick to move closer to her. Her eyes widened when he asked, "And what of us?" She started to turn back to the fire, but he stalled her with one great warm hand curled over her shoulder. "There's something between us, Tess, something powerful. Can ye deny it?"

Her mouth opened, but her answer came with difficulty. "I know there's an . . . attraction. But that's a simple thing." Her heart belied her words, thundering in her breast as he moved closer.

"An attraction, ye say?" His dark green eyes compelled her. "Aye. I would agree to that. Still, there is more. And ye know 'tis true."

"I don't think"—she wouldn't look at him as she spoke—"that it would be in my best interests to admit to that."

That puzzled him. "Whyever not?"

"What of Fiona?"

He looked startled. "That is a thing long over." When she looked doubtful, he said, "A man wants a woman who sees beyond his face or his scars, lass. I've learned that the hard way."

"She still wants you," Tess said, eyes averted.

His large warm hand grasped her chin, "But I do not want her. 'Tis you I want."

"You do?" The quivering of her bottom lip betrayed her.

It enchanted him, and he stilled it with a hungry kiss, murmuring against her lips, "Aye. I'm haunted" —he drew her lower lip into his mouth and nibbled it— "by the memory of the night we had together." A tremor swept through her, and his hands went to her cheeks as he deepened the kiss. Then he pulled away. "And I intend to have more."

His eyes full of wonder, Ian knelt before her as he had the night before. His fingers were splayed wide in a V from hip to hip. She wore a painting smock, and like the red dress of last night's fantasies it also buttoned down the front. He released button after button before he tugged the waist of her black leggings low on her hips. Slowly, he kissed the smooth, warm skin of her stomach and felt a surge of sexual response stronger than any he had ever known.

"Ach, the scent o' ye, dearling." His lips burned her with each word.

Tess gasped at the contact. He glanced up and knew she felt it too, this wild, sweeping desire.

She was lush sensuality, her expression soft, alluring.

His hands rose to the clasp between her breasts, his eyes daring her to tell him no. He looked down and peeled the pale lace cups away, watching her newly-darkened nipples harden even more. Her head fell back in surrender as his rough palms cupped her gently. A shudder ran through her, and she could hardly believe the sensitivity of her breasts.

"S'lovely ye are." His low voice thrilled her.

She gazed down at him, her eyes dark and full of sweet longing as she drank in the magnificent picture this powerful, sensual man made kneeling before her. His mouth was temptation. His eyes clearest green, his form rich muscle. He was splendid, from his dark red mane of hair to his booted feet.

"Careful," he said quickly, fighting to keep control of the hunger, its fire, thinking that there was so much unsettled between them.

"What?" she responded huskily, every nerve in her body alive with sensation.

"If you offer yourself to me like that, I'll take you." His breath rasped out. "I won't be able to resist."

Tess stared down at him for a long moment; he was telling her she could still say no. Her smile grew until it dazzled him. Her voice was husky as she said simply, "Don't resist." It seemed to her a perfect celebration of the life they had created, and she could not wait to have his heat fill her.

"We still have much to talk about." He made himself protest, though his senses were clamoring for her. He pressed his lips to her scented skin once more, his tongue finding her navel and dipping into its sensitive hollow until she made small sounds of mounting need.

Her hand trembled as it stroked over the thick, clinging waves of his hair and held him to her. "Later." She sighed. Tess told herself she didn't look for forever anymore. Each day she would accept the joys life offered.

Ian needed no more permission. In fluid motion he slipped the smock and lace straps from her shoulders. The leggings slid down to her ankles, and she stepped out of them. When she shivered, he looked up.

"Cold?" he asked her tenderly, smiling at the delicate flush that rose from her breasts to her cheeks as she shook her head no.

He leaned forward to rain kisses over her belly again as he filled his hands with the supple flesh of her buttocks. And when the wisp of pink lace got in his way, his teeth and hands tugged it downward until it, too, fell to the floor.

Knees weak, Tess grasped Ian's wide shoulders. She twisted his shirt in her hands, impatient with the material that kept her from feeling the heated texture of his skin.

Here, he thought, as he parted the warm, damp petals of flesh and blew lightly. Tess gasped, and her muscles tightened in shock. "Easy, lass." He gentled her with a kiss and whispered hoarsely, "Sweet lass, sweet Tess." He let his hot tongue stroke her, then delve deep, groaning low. *Here*, he had entered her, spending his life force, joining it with hers. He delighted in her quick sighs and panting breaths, the way she came in a crashing wave of joyous sensation.

When he stood and lifted her into his arms, Tess buried her face in his warm neck, shuddering again as she breathed deeply of his scent. By the time he took the stairs and stalked down the hall to reach her simple bedroom, she was stroking the curves of his ear with her pointed little tongue, whispering his name, sending lightning bolts of desire flooding through him.

He placed her on the bed, reluctant to release her even long enough to be rid of his clothes. But his eyes continued to caress her as he smiled a slow, sexy smile of promise.

Tess lifted one hand in a beseeching gesture that was timelessly feminine. He was beside her in the next instant, covering her with his warmth, finding her lips with his. Then came an interlude filled with slow, lush kisses that explored flavor and heat.

Tess was shaking now. "Please . . ."

"Shh, m'hinnie." Ian entered her and watched her face as he thrust deep, intensifying her pleasure. A moment later he drew back and thrust shallowly again and again.

Hands supporting the small of her back, he drew her up into a sitting position. There, he could look into her deep blue eyes, kiss her already swollen lips to an even fuller pout, and let his fingers glide over her luscious breasts. Tess leaned back until she rested her

weight on her hands behind her. In that suspended
arch she urged him on with soft, abandoned sounds.
Ian held her hips and stroked deep within her in
a rhythm that sent wild shocks of pleasure through
them both.

How she'd missed him, wanted him! And now,
here he was, buried deep inside her, rejoicing with her
in the pleasure they gave each other, and in the crea-
tion of their child. Had she ever felt such happiness?

And with that thought she found her shattering
ecstasy. He followed with a hoarse cry.

Content to lie in his strong arms, Tess basked in
the feeling of complete well-being. One of his hands
still cradled her breast, and she squirmed, loving the
friction. Then she let her fingers trace his wrist, moving up his arm in a casual caress.

"Sweet," he murmured into her hair.

"Salty," she answered with a little smile, her quick
tongue darting out to flick at his chest.

Moments passed.

"Was it awful for you in the hospital?" she asked
carefully, her eyes running over the mended cheekbone and faint lines.

"No." He sighed and let his hand slide lightly
over the rounded curve of her bottom. He squeezed,
reveling in the delicate texture he found there. "It was
the lying around I couldn't bear. I'm not a very patient
man, lassie."

"*That* ye dinna have to tell me," she mocked him,

accent and all. "Tell me about what it was like to grow up here."

The request surprised him. "I did and didn't grow up here really. I was away at school in Edinburgh during the winters, here some summers, others were spent on family holidays abroad. But there's a MacLeod reunion every four years. We were always on the Isle for that."

Her fingers played lazily through the thick red hair on his chest. "I can just see you at school—a Scottish scion, four feet tall, in little black knickers *lairding* it over all your school friends with medieval arrogance!" She laughed softly.

Ian lifted his head at the affront to stare down at her. "I am not arrogant!" he denounced.

Tess laughed again and said, "So tell me about your family."

"What d'ye wish to know? My father died when I was young. M'mother you'll meet soon enough. I've a brother and a sister. He's a doctor in the States, married to a female jockey. She's a wild sprite of a lass who keeps him on his toes. M'sister is a writer of children's books and always meddling in something or other. She uses 'the sight' as her excuse."

"The what?" Tess asked absently.

Ian let his hand slide through the whisper-soft strands of her dark hair as he answered with mock-indignation, "But ye must have heard of 'the gift' certain Scots possess!" He could see she knew nothing of it and couldn't resist teasing her, taking his voice down to a sexy drawl filled with drama. " 'Tis the ability to see the future, ye ignorant Yank, and it is as much a part of Scotland as the little people are of Ireland."

Tess smiled, her hand stilled. Her head tilted as she had a sudden notion. "Do you believe in it?"

"Mm," he answered noncommittally.

"What does that mean?" She grinned at him, pressing.

He shrugged. Looking up at his strong face, she saw his discomfort and was delighted. "You do!"

His expression betrayed a mingling of embarrassment, puzzlement, and resignation. "She's been . . . right . . . before, and there are others."

"Tell me," she said, eyes sparkling. "This sounds interesting."

His beautiful mouth moved slowly at first as he said, "It sounds idiotic, I know. I have no explanation for it." Her brows rose, and he went on. "When we were children, Kyra was always . . . finding things, things that were lost. And once, when Angus MacCrimmon and his son were adrift on the loch in a heavy fog, Kyra insisted I take her out in our skiff to find them. We did. She told me Angus had called to her."

"Angus?" She gulped. "He's psychic . . . really?"

"Aye." Ian smirked at her. "The man's famed throughout the Hebrides."

She blinked once, twice more, then propped her

chin on her hand and looked back. "And he's always right?"

When Ian said, "Well, I've never known him to be wrong," she was shocked.

"Hmmf." One slender hand played absently over the dark red curls on his chest, and she smiled. "Then, in that case, m'laird, I suppose you and I . . . will be having a son."

'Aye." He smiled down at her smugly. "So I've been told."

Her startled laughter made his eyes close in pleasure, and he held her tightly in his arms, his cheek pressed to the top of her head.

SEVEN

The first thing she did the next morning was descend on Janet and Elsbeth at the store. With the tinkling of the bell over the door, she stalked toward the counter and pinned both fairy godmothers with one purposeful glare.

Two sets of wispy brows rose in innocent surprise. Without taking her eyes from them, Tess asked, "Geordie, would you mind watching the store for a few minutes while I have a word with *Janet* and *Elsbeth* in the back?"

A newspaper rustled, a masculine throat cleared, as if wary of an impending storm, then Geordie said, "Of course, Tess. Take as long as ye like." When she heard the creak of his chair, she nodded the two, suddenly nervous women toward the back room.

Tess faced them there. "I want the truth," she said.

They blinked owlishly in response. "What have you two been up to this time?"

Janet and Elsbeth exchanged guilty glances as Janet stammered, "Wh-whatever d'ye m-mean, Tess?"

"I mean," she said, crossing her arms over her chest, "first this business with Angus making announcements about an heir for the MacLeods . . . and now an invitation to the castle for Sunday tea with her ladyship."

"Tea with Lady Aileen?" Hand fluttering, Elsbeth turned in delight to her best friend of forty years. "Did ye hear that, Janet? *Tea!*"

" 'Tis a fine way to honor all that ye've done here, lassie." Janet bobbed her head and gave a wide, relieved smile.

"That's all very well," Tess said, "but just how is it that Lady Aileen heard of . . . my condition all the way in Edinburgh? And why, do you think, would she assume my child was fathered by her son?"

The accused looked at each other in bewilderment. And Tess knew then that they'd had nothing to do with her ladyship's hasty return.

"But how else could she have known?"

Janet and Elsbeth looked at each other again and spoke at the same time. Janet sighed, "Kyra." Elsbeth sighed in echo, "Angus."

"Yes?" Tess encouraged them.

"Well, dear, about Kyra . . . she has 'the sight,' ye know," Elsbeth began carefully.

"Oh, Elsbeth, come on. You're not going to tell

me you think Angus telegraphed the news to Kyra so she'd tell her mother to hotfoot it back here?"

"Well—" Elsbeth said, shaking her head.

"Stranger things have happened," Janet chimed in, "here on the Isle of Mist."

Tess gave up and threw her hands in the air with a laugh. "So what do I wear to meet the great lady for tea?"

When Tess woke, it was late. Sometime during the night Ian had left her. She supposed he was trying to spare what was left of her reputation—though she would have liked to have someone explain the vast difference between an indiscretion and shacking up. Only a Scot would understand that one.

Tess stretched luxuriously, remembering the number of times she had been awakened in the night by his tender caresses. The last was near dawn. She had been dreaming of Ian when she woke to find him already inside her, his fingers stroking, kneading, setting her ablaze. He'd brushed her hair from her neck so that he could string little stinging bites from shoulder to shoulder. With only the second bite she had been shaking in need, arching up to meet him, desperate for deeper penetration.

Tess was pulled from the delicious memory by the realization that it was Sunday. *Tea day.* Castle day. Day of the reproachful mother. She buried her head beneath her pillow and groaned.

When Ian appeared at her door, he was in full regalia, hair flowing wild, tartan lifting in the wind at his shoulder beneath his silver brooch. His bright eyes fairly glowed at the sight of her. Tess looked him over, from the waving wine-dark hair to his hunter's jacket and sporran over his kilt of forest green, traced with red and yellow, then to his high tasseled socks.

Cute socks, she thought saucily. Hands on her hips, she lifted her chin and gave an irrepressible grin as she announced in a broad brogue, " 'Tis a fine pair of legs ye have there, laddie-o."

He felt the now-familiar fist tighten in his gut. "And 'tis a bonnie lass ye are, indeed, Tess-my-own." His voice was a little rough as he sent a wide smile back to her.

She looked down to the emerald silk dress she wore. "Will it do?"

"Aye," he answered slowly, taking in every sweet curve.

Her cheeks reddened. "Do I look pregnant?"

His smile was the one he'd met her with in the middle of the night.

"Well, there is a glow about you, hinnie, and a certain . . . lushness." Then he circled her waist with both of his great hands. "But ye're smaller here than when first I met you."

She blushed fiery red, wishing she could simply drag him back upstairs and forget the whole thing. "Should we be on our way, then?"

He looked deep into her eyes, reassuring and wondering. Finally, he murmured, "Aye," and released her. "I'll drive slow as a turtle, Tess, I promise."

She rewarded him with a gentle smile. Though it was but a two-mile drive, Tess looked at the landscape surrounding them, realizing how much she had come to love this green mist-shrouded island.

How different it was from New York's winter gray, its crowds and excitement. Here, grass rippled with the wind, and mist feathered the land like a lover's touch that came and went. The sea was a beauteous, living view, and each loch and village had a character all its own. Herds of sheep had the run of the narrow winding roads, led by rams with bells round their necks that traveled where fancy led. They made her laugh.

On Skye the stories weren't of nameless, faceless people, but people she saw every day. Those faces had become very dear to her. Their special humor and care for one another touched something deep within her.

Strange, she thought, for someone who had deliberately and completely isolated herself to become so involved in a community.

They were coming up to the castle now, and the weathered gray stone of its high walls and rounded towers was terribly imposing. The open gates held an ancient Celtic sign in a circle of gold amid the black iron bars. The winding paths of the garden lay to one side of the long drive.

Ian drove down and around to the lower bailey. A thick wooden door there was open. Tess got out of the car and glanced around her at the high turrets and loch beyond. It was quite a romantic sight.

"How wonderful." She sighed. "But you don't wish to live here, Ian?"

" 'Tis the family residence and m'mother's home. When I finished university and felt I needed a place of my own, Aileen gave me the loan of the dower house. Someday, I'll live here. It will be soon enough," he finished in a quiet voice as he stared up at the castle.

Tess understood the implication and followed his gaze. "I feel it now, the responsibility you have to your family and the Isle. It fills the air here, like centuries of tradition." She grinned irreverently and said, "Just a small anvil above your head."

"Aye," Ian answered simply, his expression softening as he looked around in proud possession. His gaze met hers. "But there are compensations. And that connection extends to all the family, including the wee laddie lying beneath your heart." He gave her a steady look that shook her, even before he continued with, "And yourself."

The words brought another bright blush to her cheeks. He was chiseling away at her convictions of independence with each day that passed. She'd have to learn to be more on her guard or she might find herself wrapped in that tartan, her life rearranged in a world of duty and nannies, designer hats, polo, and dull parties with forced conversation.

Ian sensed her withdrawal and placed a hand on the small of her back. Even through her coat she felt its warmth. "Come along then, this way."

They were met by a man who so resembled Ranald that Tess couldn't help but show her surprise. "Laird Ian, miss." The man gave a small bow of his head.

Ian grinned. "Ms. Tess Hartley, this is Andrew, also a MacLeod, brother of Ranald. He cares for all at Castle Dunvegan."

Tess smiled easily. "How nice to meet you, Andrew. I am very fond of your brother. He does so much for us at the center."

Andrew let a hint of a twinkle light his amber eyes. "Ranald speaks very highly of ye also, miss. Especially yer early attempts to learn to play shinty."

Tess laughed delightedly. "Ranald liked seeing me swing so hard I rolled to the bottom of the hill, that's all. It seems your brother enjoys having people look up to him," she finished with a grin. "Perhaps you'll join us one evening at the center. There's chess, even card games." Then she lowered her voice and looked toward Ian as if he might be a secret constable. "Though we don't play for money, of course."

"Of course, miss." Andrew pursed his lips.

"What is this new madness?" Ian scowled. "Shinty, of all things! 'Tis a rough pub sport, Tess! Ye might have been seriously harmed!"

Andrew watched with great interest as Tess laid her hand on the laird's arm and gave him a lovely smile. "I begged Ranald to show me the basics and wound up entertaining both teams with my clumsiness. That was months ago, Ian. Truly, I'm very careful now."

But Ian was busy muttering, "What could Ranald have been thinking of, I wonder? And what other hair-raising tales have been kept from me? This will take some looking into." He grimaced and pointed for Andrew to proceed them up the stairs to the entrance hall.

Tess only chuckled and followed his lead. "Well, he did nearly skewer me with a dart once," she teased, quite unable to resist. "But what I'm really eager to learn is the sword dance. Will you teach me?"

Andrew smothered a snort of laughter as Ian gave a low growl of frustration and stamped up the stairs.

Ian formally presented Tess to the ladies Aileen and Kyra MacLeod as they stood beside the massive stone fireplace. Tess blinked in surprise, for the family resemblance was very strong, although Lady Aileen's strawberry-blond hair and delicate features had turned to fiery auburn and stronger contours in her children. The gemstone-green eyes blazed from the face of each of the MacLeods.

Lady Aileen gave Tess a winning smile, remarking, "Do you know, I have seen your work in the home of friends in Paris, Ms. Hartley? I believe that you are extraordinarily gifted."

Tess was surprised by both the compliment and the warmth with which it was delivered when she had expected challenge and ultimatum. She sent a shy glance to a beaming Ian as Aileen mentioned a few acquaintances in the New York art world.

Meanwhile, Ian bent to press a kiss of hello to Kyra's cheek and whispered a question. "Is it you I have to thank for this occasion then, bratling?"

Kyra whispered back, "Shame on ye, Ian. Ye know I never interfere."

The look he returned was a patent reproach, but Kyra merely blinked demurely and continued aloud, "Mairie has made yer raisin scones, Ian."

"Are they a favorite?" Tess smiled and asked.

"Aye." Kyra laughed. "When he was a boy, Ian's pockets were always full of scones he'd filched from the kitchen while Mairie the cook pretended not to notice. He was always her favorite, the beast, even when he put stones in the porridge and sand in the gravy."

"Careful, Kie," Ian warned darkly, the affection clear in his voice. "The tales of yer own childhood devilment abound."

"Our Ian has to be very careful of his dignity these days." Kyra stuck her pretty nose into the air as she leaned forward and whispered loudly with an affected, casual tone, "He's the laird, you know." The comment reminded them all of the reason behind this meeting and created an abrupt silence until Aileen poured the tea.

The room was immense, with dark rafters high above and a view of the loch. Glowing wood, antiques upholstered in Victorian tapestries, and great vases filled with flowers made the room warmly welcoming.

"I understand you've made startling improvements in the lives of our villagers, Ms. Hartley," Aileen finally began.

"Please, call me Tess, Your Ladyship."

"And I am Aileen." Ian's mother smiled and asked more questions about the center. Tess answered with pleasure. However, each moment that they avoided the inevitable subject of her pregnancy, she was becoming more and more apprehensive.

Ian's mother was far too kind to be told to mind her own business. Still, Tess couldn't imagine another response if Aileen demanded participation in her decision.

At last the lady turned to Ian and said, "Ian dear, there are some . . . papers in the study that should be brought to your attention. Kyra, would you show him the parcel from Edinburgh?"

Ian lifted one brow. "As much as I love ye, sweet

Aileen, I am no' leaving ye to make mischief with my lass."

"Please, Ian," Tess asked softly, the words "my lass" echoing again and again in her head. "For just a few minutes. I'd like to speak to your mother alone."

He stared at her and finally nodded his consent. Turning to his sister, he said, "Come along then, bratling," and strode impatiently from the room.

"My son cares for you," Aileen said quietly, taking Tess's hand in her own soft one. "That much is clear."

"He's been very kind to me," Tess returned.

Aileen lifted a brow. "Kind."

"And . . . we do have . . . a r-relationship that is very special," Tess stammered.

Aileen frowned lightly. "But you do not wish a . . . permanent arrangement with Ian despite your relationship?" The green eyes were very gentle but very perceptive.

"I was married, Your Ladyship—"

"Aileen."

"Yes, I'm sorry, Aileen." Tess wished she knew how to continue.

"I am a widow also, Tess. I know what it is to grieve for the man you love. But I've watched you look at my son, and I see genuine affection for him in your eyes."

"We hardly know each other . . . and we're very different."

"Perhaps you might consider an engagement to start."

Tess gave a vehement shake of her head and stared at her hands, now twisting in her lap.

Ian's mother took a slow sip of tea and set her cup down. Then she turned to face Tess completely. "Do you know what the British press will do to my son and his child in print?" Her voice hardened a bit, and Tess could see that this woman had the strength to be a formidable foe. "They'll dredge up the story of his mutilated face and body. The front page will have sensationalized pictures of the two of you and stories of your 'love child'. Reporters will swarm over the Isle. Then, when the bairn comes, they'll start it all again."

Tess swallowed hard. "If I must, I can leave, go back to America."

"And take his child from him?" Aileen rose and went to the wide mullioned windows. Her delicate hand smoothed over the brocade draperies and then came to rest upon the rope sash that held them. "Ian doesn't like to speak of it, but he was with his father the day he died. He was very young and almost lost his own life to the sea trying to save Lackie when he was swept overboard. Of course Ian blamed himself; he would. His father had taught him that to be the MacLeod heir was to hold the responsibility for everything and everyone MacLeod. When Lackie died, Ian believed he'd failed us all. He became anoth-

YOU GET SIX ROMANCES RISK FREE...
Plus AN EXCLUSIVE TITLE FREE!

Loveswept Romances

6 ROMANCES RISK FREE

Kay Hooper's
Larger Than Life

This FREE gift is yours to keep.

MY "NO RISK" GUARANTEE

There's no obligation to buy and the free gift is mine to keep. I may preview each subsequent shipment for 15 days. If I don't want it, I simply return the books within 15 days and owe nothing. If I keep them, I will pay just $2.25 per book. I save $3.00 off the retail price for the 6 books (plus postage and handling, and sales tax in NY).

YES! Please send my six Loveswept novels RISK FREE along with my FREE GIFT described inside the heart! CB2   41228

NAME_____

ADDRESS_____ APT_____

CITY_____

STATE_____ ZIP_____

Prices subject to change. Orders subject to approval.

er person then, wild and unreachable, angry somehow."

Aileen's head was bowed, and her slender back was ramrod-straight. Her posture bespoke great pain. "He spent his money on nothing that gave back—parties and mistresses, reckless adventures. Then, when he was so horribly injured, he made himself an outcast, though others called him hero. He wouldn't even let his family near." She stopped for a moment, her voice a bit unsteady.

Tess felt her own throat close and wished she knew what to say. Ian hadn't told her any of this, and that, too, hurt.

Aileen took a deep breath. "Those were very dark times. But they're over . . . Ian's different now. I've my son back, Tess." She turned and gave Tess a look that seemed to sear through her like a knife. "He's become a man I admire as well as love. Even from hospital in Edinburgh, he was conducting clan business: high finance, estate management, charitable donations. I wonder, my dear, how much of that difference is due to his accident and how much is due to you." The lady smiled. "Now, Ian has fathered a child and . . . this thing of great joy could become another sorrow for my laddie to bear." Tears sparkling in the liquid depths of her eyes, she whispered slowly, her heart in each word, "I would do anything you ask to keep that from happening, Tess. Anything."

❖―――――❖

The mist slipped around the car in the early dark like a quiet caress. The colors were muted, softest grays and black touched with pale wisps of fog. The scent of the sea was strong.

"Are ye well, Tess?" Ian asked as the castle disappeared behind them in evening's darkness. "Ye seemed quite pale as we left."

"I'm fine." But the answer came in a voice so small that Ian pulled off the road entirely and took her chin in his hand. "Tears now?"

Her breath huffed out. "Really, Ian. Your mother was wonderful. I . . . I cry all the time these days. . . . It has nothing to do with anything."

He smiled gently, sadly. "Ah, don't cry, m'lass." He held her face and kissed away the trickling tears. "We'll find some way to make it all come all right." And his arms came around her.

The days passed happily for Tess. Christmas was just a week away, and the center bustled with preparations. Her own work was going well. She had managed to complete three paintings, though she kept being drawn back to the portrait of Ian that somehow she could not finish.

Tess wasn't a woman for closed doors, and there were times she felt Ian watching her at work. She would stand at her easel and lift her hair or tilt her head in consideration. She would feel his presence and look up to find him standing in the doorway, his expression intent, unreadable.

Still, when their gazes met, he would nod as if he had simply come to the cottage to check on her. If she didn't offer to stop and have tea or lunch, he would quietly slip away again. He was *around*, though he never intruded upon her work or demanded to see what she painted. She thought it very dear of him. She wouldn't have believed a man so imperious could be intuitive as well. Little did he know that it was the landscape with his own portrait that occupied so much of her time.

He did continue to insist that Callie come five days a week to cook and clean so that Tess would be free to do her own work. And Tess was grateful, though she didn't know a way to show Ian.

It seemed that she was tired so often, painting only three or four hours before she needed to nap. When she woke, she rushed to the center where she spent another three hours before walking home. Ian had volunteered to drive her countless times, but she insisted that she and the baby needed the exercise. Once home, she would set her small table, and Ian would appear to share the dinner Callie had prepared.

They ate together most nights and learned more about each other as they spoke of the day's work.

Though she didn't talk about her painting, Tess told him of the goings-on at the center: how Betty's cooking class had attracted students from as far away as Kyleakin and how Andrew had finally consented to teach a class in Gaelic. In turn, Ian told her about the circuit of tenants he visited. He'd already explained the trouble over the bridge and his attempts to minimize the ill feeling while doing a bit of investigation on the side.

Under the guise of a friendly pint or two, he'd give advice on husbandry and vitamins for the sheep and sometimes lend a hand with farm repairs or take the time to discuss the bridge and what it would mean to all those on the Isle. Some groused about the need for the bridge and extra commerce, and others expressed their fear that it would turn Skye into a Scots Disneyworld, where tourists would overrun their land and force them from their own homes to build summer getaways.

Then came two more incidents. A shop in Portree was vandalized, graffiti sprayed over counters and goods. And, deep in the night, young Blair's automobile was set ablaze in his drive. Some said it was retaliation.

If there was an issue in Scotland, Ian told her, it was debated in the pubs with a variety of opinions and a great deal of passion. And the climate in the pubs was getting decidedly dangerous.

Tess tried to ignore the sharp pang of fear that

struck through her when she imagined Ian going up against those who were capable of such violence. But he seemed to feel it his duty to root out the trouble-makers himself.

They dried dishes together that night, and Ian felt a familiar heat spread through his veins as Tess reached high and bent forward to put a serving dish in the cupboard over the counter.

Her dark hair slid over her shoulders in sensuous motions. The plump curve of her behind brought him to an instant state of arousal, and one of his big hands moved forward to follow that sweet line before the thought had even formed in his mind.

Tess felt the warmth of his caress and blushed as his thumb rode the back seam of her jeans and slid downward. She felt the soft press of his lips against her sensitive nape. It raised tiny hairs there, and she sighed, letting her eyes close in pleasure. Arching her back, Tess felt his other hand cup her breast. Magic. There was such magic in his touch.

"You will be careful, won't you, Ian?" she said softly, feeling a sweet cloud of passion overwhelm her.

"D'ye worry for me, then, lassie?" He gave her a nibbling bite, pleased at her sign of feeling for him, for she'd never shown another.

She didn't answer but turned her head and found his lips with a hunger that had only begun to burn. The warm, sweet scent of her sent a shiver of arousal through him. He could have kissed her forever, but his hands moved over her with a will of their own. Her breasts were exquisite, like ripe peaches: full, and heavy in his palms.

He pulled her to the kitchen table and cleared it with a single swipe of his arm.

"Ian!" she protested. "Oh"—her protest turned to a sigh as her head fell back—"oh, Ian . . ."

EIGHT

He let one hand give an absent stroke over the silken skin of her hip. She was so beautiful, tempting and voluptuous with his child. Three months gone now, there wasn't much time left for him to convince her to marry him.

"*Tha gaol agam ort, m'sidh*," he whispered low.

"What did you say?" Tess settled herself against his warm shoulder, sleepy, smiling whimsically at the lilting sound of his words.

Relaxed, Ian placed his hand behind his head. A sated smile on his face, he asked, "Ye wish to hear it again, then?" At her nod he sat up, and put both hands around her waist to caress the gentle swell of her new belly as he whispered, "I love ye, m'fairy lass." His mouth teased her sensitive earlobe. "And well ye know it."

"No!" She sat up quickly.

"No?" Ian blinked, his arms tightening, then sliding slowly away to turn her shoulders to him.

"No, please." Tess rose from the bed and reached for her robe, belting it with crisp motions. As she pulled her hair free, she announced, "I don't want you to . . . feel that way about me."

"And how did ye plan to stop it?" he asked, angry, incredulous, throwing back the covers in a furious motion.

"Don't, Ian." She turned slowly back to him. "I don't have that in me. I can't return those feelings. The price is too high. I don't even think I believe in things like permanence and fidelity anymore." She looked him straight in the eye and said, "I no longer put my faith in promises. Too many things can go wrong, no matter what we think is going to happen. I know that Ben loved me, and if he could . . . could leave me, anyone could. But that doesn't mean I have to set myself up again. And I won't."

"Your husband didn't leave ye—he died!"

"It's the same in the end." Her eyes were so sad that they tore him apart. "And I don't want to be left again. One day you'll wake up and want your old life back, and the women who went with it. And you'll see that I wouldn't fit into that life. But you won't have any trouble finding someone else, Ian. Women fall all over themselves for you."

A few moments passed, then he spoke in a low,

deliberate voice. "Ye have dealt me an insult I wouldna take from any man or woman." He turned in a slow whirl and sent her a dark glare. "Ye question my ethics, my loyalty. Nay, ye dinna question. Ye state yer certain doubt! And am I supposed to take that easily?"

Shaken by the depth of his anger, Tess said, just above a whisper, "That's the point, Ian. I am not asking you for anything."

"Aye, Tess," he said in a slow, sad monotone. "You're right. There lies the difficulty. Ye won't take, and ye won't give . . . at least no more than the pleasure of your sweet white body. I don't care to think of what that makes of what we share."

"Ian!" Devastated, she looked into his eyes. She reached up to stroke his cheek, then slipped her fingers through his auburn hair. He seemed to have turned to stone. Tess wouldn't have thought she could have such an impact on him. "I wouldn't hurt you—"

"Then why do ye?" he interrupted gruffly, staring over her shoulder.

Tess was astounded. She had never expected such a statement from Ian. Since he had returned after the last operations, he'd seemed invincible.

"How?" she asked, turning her shocked gaze to his.

"Yer bloody indifference! What d'ye think?"

"You think I'm indifferent?" She couldn't believe what he was saying. "You get within two feet of me, and I begin to tremble! I've never been so affected by a man in my life!"

"And ye keep every real emotion to yerself, hoarding your feelings like an old woman with the last crust of bread and no hope!" His voice was raised, his face darkly flushed. She could even see the muscles tighten in his jaw as he fought to control himself.

Never had she seen him so angry. It was frightening. Still, she stood straight and faced him. "Exactly what is it that you want from me, Ian? Can you tell me that?"

"I want more than a damned mistress, that's for certain!" he roared. "I want ye to care for me more than ye fear whatever it is that makes ye hold yourself from me!" He grabbed her shoulders, not realizing that his fingers bruised her. "Why do ye do it, Tess? I know ye care. I see it in your eyes when I come through the door. I feel it in the sweet sound of your cries when I love you. Why do ye hide so, damn ye?" She struggled in his arms. "Why do ye run and then push at me s'hard that I'm sure to leave ye?" He gave her a single hard shake, as if he could force the emotion from her. Finally, she began to struggle in his arms.

Trapped, hating his words, Tess tossed back her head and suddenly knew a rage she'd never felt before. Her vision clouded, and her arms snapped up to throw his hands away. "No, damn you! You can't have it!" She wanted to hit him, but she reached for the vase of roses he'd given her, throwing it against the wall with a curse of helpless fury. "Whatever I had was his!" she cried out, the words coming without thought from someplace deep within her. "I won't give everything and have it taken away again! I won't, and nothing you can do can make me!" she finished childishly.

"Bloody hell, woman! Are ye daft?" Ian bellowed back. "I dinna wish to leave you. I wish to marry you!"

Tess could only stand and shake her head hopelessly, her eyes dry, heart hollow, as she looked away from his beautiful face and glittering eyes. Finally, Ian reached for his pants, and Tess realized that he'd been stark naked while they had had a screaming match loud enough to call out the clan.

Her hands pulled at each other as she went to the window. She listened to the rustling whispers that came as he jerked on his clothing and stamped into his boots. She caught the sound of each footstep that took him from her room and down the stairs, then the resounding crash of the front door.

And at last there was no sound but the drumming of her own panicked heart.

Ian tramped up *Halabhal Bheag*. Along with *Healabhal Mor*, the twin flat-topped mountains were known as MacLeod's Tables. This was his private place.

His expression as fierce as any warring laird of old, he climbed with Duke, tartan blowing about him in the high wind. His chin raised in defiance; his teeth ground together with each step.

Tess was slipping through his fingers, and he knew of no way to stop her. Aye, she painted now and laughed and knew the pleasures his body could give to hers. But there was that wall behind her eyes that never crumbled, even when she cried his name in the dark of night. And what of the babe? Would she withhold her love from their son as well?

He sat on the high crag, one hand resting in Duke's soft fur as he stared bleakly over the land. He had a fine view of Glendale and the winding bit of road to Dunvegan, as well as the loch itself. The whiteness of the sheep in winter coats against the green grass and silver boulders soothed his senses, as the sight of his own castle reminded him of things his people had accomplished, against all odds, throughout the centuries. If serenity was to be had, he usually found it here.

Suddenly, he heard the soft humming of a woman's voice and knew without turning that it could only be Kyra. Standing behind him, she wrapped her arms around his great shoulders and laid her cheek against his rough one.

"An' what do ye here in all this wind, *brathair mo*?"

She'd coaxed a bit of a smile as he clasped her

arms with his own. "Aye, only a brother would put up with yer interfering ways. So did ye follow me to keep me from catching a chill then?"

She sighed and moved to sit beside him on the great rock. "I heard yer heart call over the moor."

The bitter smile turned whimsical. "But it was not ye I called, my wee bird."

Her small hand covered his great one, and her voice was quiet as she said, "I know." Her head leaning on her brother's shoulder, the auburn of her hair tangling with his, Kyra began to sing softly. It was a tune their mother had often sung to them in the nursery; it was Aileen's favorite.

With a haunting lilt of memory the story told of Ian, fourth chief of the MacLeods, who had chanced to come upon a fairy princess in the wood. The bold, proud chief and the enchanting lady fell deeply and immediately in love. They married and were splendidly happy until, one misty night, after twenty years, the fairies called their princess back to them. It was a summons she could not dismiss. And though it broke both their hearts, Ian's love left him at the place known forever after as the Fairy Bridge.

The modern-day Ian remembered how, as much as sweet Aileen had loved the romance of the story, she had never been able to bear the ending. So she created another verse in which the MacLeod charmed his fairy wife.

In her version every lonely night after the fairy

wife was taken from Ian, he returned to that bridge and played his harp with such haunting sadness that the fairies finally brought her back to him, knowing that they had become too much a part of each other to be separated. And when she appeared before Ian out of the mist, her eyes wet with human tears, she vowed that nothing would ever again separate them. "The fairies have proclaimed it," she announced, smiling at her beloved. And so it was.

There, on *Halabhal Bheag*, Ian joined Kyra in that final verse. Their voices blended and filled the cool air with melody. A quiet came, and a solemn peace, as it seemed even the wind died down to listen.

"We had best start back before the mist rises," Kyra finally said. "I fear we'll need the compass even now."

"Och, aye," Ian answered, and gave Duke a last scratch behind the ears. "Although finding his way back to his bowl seems to be this animal's single useful talent. Come away, Duke."

Kyra knew well her brother's protective instincts. He probably gave the animal half his dinner each night. "Ian," she said, with a mysterious smile, "do see that ye remember the motto MacLeod."

Ian made a sound that might have been a laugh. "Aye, ye she-witch. 'Twas that I was thinking of just before ye found me here." He took her arm and pressed it to his own. He looked down to her sweet, familiar face, and he took a deep breath. Their voices rang out together through the glen. "*Hold fast!*" Then they laughed, for it had been a childhood trick. "But this battle may demand the use of the *fairy flag* itself afore we're through!"

Christmas came to Tess with the warmth of new friends and a rain of handmade gifts. Ranald brought her a small tree, and she forced herself to hang it with cranberries and popcorn, peppermint canes, and the small twinkling lights she had so adored as a child.

But there was no Ian.

He and Tess had planned to spend Christmas Eve in front of the fire and the next day at the castle. Instead, Tess rocked alone before her fire, gently caressing her stomach as she hummed along to the carols on the radio. Duke seemed to have adopted either her fireplace or herself for the holidays. She believed animals had a sensitivity to human emotion, but of course the extra treats she gave him might have had a bit to do with his keeping close.

At ten o'clock Duke ran for the door and sniffed, wagging his tail, making her heart race. She walked slowly to the door, waiting, listening. Finally, when she couldn't stand it anymore, she threw it open. But no one was there.

Disappointed, she began to close the door again.

Then she saw it. Small and square, the box on the steps was wrapped in shiny red paper and topped with mistletoe.

"Ian." She sighed and looked out into the darkness, but there was no one in sight; she saw only the swirling mist.

Inside, she sank into her rocker, cradling the gift and blinking away tears. Finally she found the courage to open it. It was a small gold pendant encrusted with tiny diamonds, carved in the shape of a thistle, an early symbol of Scotland.

Her fingers ran over and over the delicate shape as she stared into the fire. Then she went upstairs, placed it in her jewelry box, and closed the lid.

Christmas Day she was dragged down to the center by Janet and Elsbeth for a caroling party. She had already spoken to her brother in New York. This Christmas season, her father was in Switzerland and, as usual, unreachable.

Just as well, she told herself. She wasn't a very good liar, and Michael read her like a book.

Life went on with comforting patterns. She painted and taught her classes. She was delighted to find them increasing and filled with quite a few talented individuals. Her growing child taxed her body but buoyed her spirits. Just as her students grew used to her dashing from the hall with "morning sickness" that was never so predictable as to occur only in the mornings, the phenomenon suddenly stopped. She let Janet and Elsbeth take over the craft exports, and the sewing class created a maternity wardrobe for her.

She was keeping a low profile with her social life, more than content to invite a select few to tea or an occasional dinner. So far, the press had left her quite alone.

Gossip had it that Ian was living in Edinburgh, and though she missed him terribly, she supposed it was just as well. Though she hadn't responded to his Christmas gift, more packages arrived every few days. First came a book of poetry, Robert Burns. Then a box of chocolates. The third gift was hand-delivered by Ranald. He stood on her front steps in his kilt. When she opened the door, he bowed and presented her with a beautifully wrapped MacLeod tartan, saying, "For the mother of the heir."

Each gift chipped a bit of her protective shell until she thought she'd go crazy if Ian didn't come home soon.

She did receive regular phone calls from sweet Aileen but always managed to excuse herself from the invitations to tea or dinner. Tess knew the Lady MacLeod would do everything in her power to sway her, and with her hormones keeping her in an emotional uproar, Tess felt she had to avoid that exposure at all costs.

————◆————————◆————

It was mild in February, much warmer than in the south, because of the location of the island to warming tides or some such. They had their share of gales and mist, however, and Ranald had taken to driving her to the center every day against all protests.

Her pregnancy five-and-a-half months along, she felt better than she had felt in her life. The morning sickness was gone, and she could still move about fairly easily. She had turned to Betty Doon's yoga for exercise, and there was a euphoria she hadn't remembered from her last pregnancy. She laughed at herself when she realized that she had become inordinately fond of the parlor rocker and the tapes her brother sent her from New York for her VCR.

She had just risen from that seat to make herself a cup of tea when a great pounding sounded at her door. Frowning, she wondered if there was trouble. What she saw when she opened it was just that.

Tess gulped. "Michael!" Well over six feet, her silver-haired father dominated the doorway, his mac dripping as he glowered at her with the brusque diplomacy of any Scot, although his own ancestry was Boston Irish.

"What in the name of heaven are you doing here?" she demanded, hands on her hips. "I just heard you were climbing some Swiss mountain!"

"Well, I *am* your father, Tess!" the giant huffed. "Did you think I'd forget my only girl . . . though she swore her brother to secrecy when she disappeared? And by the way, he only told when I threatened to hire a detective agency." He made a sound of annoyance and shook his head. "How long did you expect to stay hidden from your loving family!"

Dear, blustering Michael, she thought as she gave a silent laugh and an audible sigh. She should have known he'd unearth her whereabouts. The man was a natural detective. "Not without good reason, Pop," she tried to mollify him as she ushered his rain-sodden bulk in toward the fire.

Reaching high for his coat, she then settled him into a great comfortable chair at the fire when she caught his sudden stare at her girth. With another sigh she moved to get him a brandy. "We have things to talk about, as you can see. I'll go make some tea." She dearly needed a moment to regroup.

The ritual calmed her, and she smiled to think that she was so loved, her father would track her down across all of Europe. They'd spoken, of course, during the time she'd been here, but she had made it seem as if she were traveling about on an extended vacation. She, like Ian, hadn't been very open to family interference through her difficulties. Michael and she hadn't been close when she was young. But his persistence showed his unfailing care for her. And he would care for his grandchild.

She grinned for the first time in days at the thought of his blowhard reaction. She carried the tea tray into the parlor with a smile, her eyes on her footing as she searched for the right words. Her way was the direct way. It always had been, and it wasn't changing now. So she took a deep breath. "I'm afraid I've really gotten myself in trouble this time, Pop. I mean . . . the sixties-movies-with-Connie Stevens kind of trouble."

"So I have just been informed by this gentleman, Tess," Michael answered grimly from his chair. "Of course, he seems to have the impression that you would have taken your father into your confidence." Tess would have dropped the tray if Ian hadn't taken it from her to set it safely down upon the coffee-table.

"However did you . . . ?" Her arms fell limply to her sides as she stared up into the searing green of his eyes. "No." She almost smiled before she straightened her features. "Let me guess. Was it Kyra or Angus this time?"

Ian did look guilty. He opened his mouth, but Tess whirled to Michael before he could begin an explanation.

"They seem to have some kind of, ah, network here on the Isle, Pop. It's really very interesting if you look at it from a scientific point of view." She smoothed her hair back behind her right ear.

It was a gesture of discomfort Michael recognized from her childhood. Her cheeks burned too. This man meant something to his Tess, for she hadn't been so visibly affected since Ben. Michael mentally rubbed his hands together. He'd soon see the lay of the land, and he had the future of his grandchild to attend to now.

"A network, you say. Well . . ." Michael stood to pour out another brandy and hand it to Ian, who looked flushed as well. "That might be a welcome thing. I don't believe I would mind a few answers. I seem to have been put off with half-truths for some time."

Ian took the brandy and the chair Michael gestured to on the opposite side of the fireplace. "Whatever ye wish to know, sir." He sat back, then shifted forward, the snifter held in both hands, his fingers moving it round and round.

"Pop," Tess protested, her full lips pressed tightly together, "I think I'd like to speak with you in private before this discussion goes any further."

Michael began ominously, "According to Mr. MacLeod—"

"Um . . . it's . . . Laird MacLeod, Pop," Tess interrupted nervously before she glanced at Ian. Strange, the more agitated she became, the calmer he seemed.

Michael gave Ian a raised brow and a nod of acknowledgment. Then he huffed. "According to . . . the laird, here, he is the father of my *soon-to-be* grandchild . . . *about* whom I have never received a single word . . . not by letter, telephone, or *pony express!*" Michael was working himself into a fine, quiet rage, and, as usual, his control working against that temper was a sight to see. Tess recognized a tic starting near his left eye.

"Now, Pop . . ." She grabbed the edge of the sofa while she tried to think of something that might calm her father.

"Mr. Ryan," the laird began, reaching for the sense of authority that would, most probably, be his only weapon against this most formidable gentleman. "Tess really shouldn't be upset at this time."

The woman in question stared at him in horror before she bent double and put her forehead in her hand. Taking a position of power right in front of her father? Michael would have a seizure!

With perfect timing there came another knock on the door.

"Oh, Lord!" Tess moaned to the floor, muttering, "Who's left, the queen mother?"

She wasn't terribly far off, as it turned out. Ian went to the door, acting as if he owned the place, damn him! There, he found the Lady Aileen with Kyra in tow.

Tess rolled her eyes and announced, to no one in particular, "We'll certainly need more tea," before she jumped up to escape to the kitchen with a toss of her dark hair and an unconsciously feminine swing to her hips.

Tess cursed when she burned her palm at the stove and found her hand taken by one that was small and white. Looking up in panic, she saw that it was Kyra.

"Softly, Tess." The auburn-haired beauty squeezed her hand gently. Kyra gave a quick sigh. "Sweet Aileen means ye no harm."

"Why do you call her that, you and Ian?" Tess asked curiously, her deep blue eyes looking down to their joined hands. But she was thinking, if she could only distract Kyra, she could survive a few more minutes pretending this night wasn't happening.

Kyra smiled at the memory and put her other hand over the burn. Tess found that Kyra's touch was hot, but strangely it didn't hurt. On the contrary, it seemed soothing to the burn.

" 'Twas my father's name for her, unless they were raging at each other. They did have battles royal. And then it was 'dearling' he called her, whether in anger or bliss." She gave a small chuckle. "It must have been effective, for they were happy. Very happy."

Tess was suddenly distracted. "Kyra, my burn . . ."

Ian's sister looked down and smiled. "Aye, there are times it works that way. I would that it had for Ian." She seemed angry for a moment. "I had no help for him." She moved to turn off the stove as Tess stared at her. "But would ye two have met then, and shared what ye did, I wonder?"

All pain had disappeared from Tess's fingers, the redness as well. She stammered out a "Thank you," and Kyra smiled.

"He loves ye, Tess, whether ye ken or not."

Tess was quiet a moment before she spoke softly. "What Ian wants carries too high a price."

"Well," Kyra answered, "that, of course, is your decision to make. I believe there are some things that are worth the price. But Ian is forever telling me I meddle too much."

Introductions had obviously been made by the time Tess and Kyra returned to the parlor. Aileen was sipping brandy, and Michael was looking at her as if she were a treasure of great price.

Ian was reading a newspaper with an avid quality that immediately called her attention. Other papers were spread over the coffee table. He looked up when she and Kyra entered. He gathered the newspapers toward him, as if he were simply clearing a space for the tea tray, but Tess had already seen the paparazzi photos of Ian and herself.

Unfortunately, Aileen had been right in her predictions. Someone had leaked the story to the papers.

Tess felt a momentary flash of pain that among the people she had come to care for in this village, there was one who meant her harm. They had shared so much.

Kyra set down the tray, and Ian passed her a brandy. Tess sat upon the one remaining chair, the rocker, and steeled herself.

"You might as well let me see them now," she said to Ian. "I'll need to know what I'm up against."

Silent, he handed them over. They were every bit as appalling as Aileen had warned her they would be. Freedom of the press. In Great Britain it seemed the dailies were more tabloid than news, damn them.

One article was particularly virulent, parading her past as if she had captured one of their very own aristocracy by devious means because there was such a tragic void in her life. It referred to the fact that she was a painter who had lived as a "bohemian" until she'd married. Then the papers went into lurid detail about the accident and stated that, although Tess Hartley was very well received as an artist in both Europe and the States, she hadn't produced any paintings since the tragedy. She had come to Skye, they reported, to start a community center at Dunvegan. The article made it appear that she saw the center as the quickest way to the laird's money and heart. It also used his former fiancée Fiona Blair, as a major source for verification.

She looked up at Ian, blinking back tears, and found him watching her. "How could they say such things and know so many details? They've made our lives so ugly! How do I respond to this?"

He held her gaze and determined, "Ye need say nothing, dearling."

"Nay, Ian. Tess will wish the truth." Aileen looked right into her eyes. "Ian doesna wish to worry you, sweetheart. But the truth is that they will descend upon us . . . tomorrow or the next day," Ian's mother cautioned her. "They'll be looking for your reaction to give them more publicity."

"She'll stay at the dower house with me until things die down," Ian proclaimed, all lord of the manor once again.

"I certainly will not!" Tess said hotly.

"I can protect my own daughter from a few reporters." Michael raised his jaw in masculine determination.

"I don't think you realize, Michael." Aileen spoke in a soft, refined voice, but her message was definitive. "There will not be one or two but hordes of them. They will photograph every movement from the house, and from every window, even bedroom windows." She looked into the dark blue eyes so like his daughter's. "They cannot have accessibility to her." Then she smiled in a way that lit her face and warmed his heart. "Our grandchild is at stake."

"You have a suggestion, Aileen?" Michael asked.

The lady nodded regally. "Castle Dunvegan. In the last seven centuries the MacLeods have held off far more dangerous threats than newspeople. All we need do is close the gates. Or if that fails, Andrew is quite practiced at fending off unwanted intruders."

Tess was incredulous. "Do you think I plan to imprison myself in your castle? I'll simply find another cottage."

"And they will find you," Aileen said definitely.

"It will take time. But staying at the castle is the best way to discourage this publicity and its problems. It shouldn't take much more than a few weeks."

Tess stood up. "Aileen, you are making me feel that you're trying to force me to marry Ian, and you're using this publicity to do it!"

"Tess!" Aileen's voice was quiet, her gaze direct. "You'll be asked to do naught ye dinna wish." She came to put her hand on Tess's shoulder. "For now, our thoughts are on your health and that of the bairn. Ye ken?"

Tears sprang to her eyes, and Tess bent her head, then nodded.

"Michael, you are also invited," Aileen said, her brogue controlled once more. "We've many a room, and you can stay as long as you like. I'm sure it would help Tess to have you there."

Michael nodded solemnly and watched his daughter. He noticed again the changes in her body, and his heart still thundered at the thought of his child having a baby. He had felt this way once before, but then tragedy of such proportions had struck that he still felt only fury. He didn't care if this baby was illegitimate or heir to a sultan's throne, he wanted peace and happiness for his daughter and grandchild. Those feelings were a product of his age, perhaps. But the idea of holding his child's child in his arms made him feel a joy he could hardly begin to understand. It was nature, he supposed.

Ian never took his gaze from Tess. Finally, he said, "I'd like a moment alone with Tess."

"Oh, God," Tess murmured under her breath to her shoes.

Michael walked up to Ian and said softly, "Mind the child and how upset she's been."

Ian pulled away to look into Michael's eyes and say, "They have my love, Michael, and will always get all m'care."

Michael turned in a full arc. "May I take you to dinner, Lady Aileen?" His blue eyes twinkled across the room.

"Ah, no. I've a grand feast waiting at the castle, Mr. Ryan. Kyra and I would greatly enjoy your company."

Michael grinned, feeling his senses come alive. "If you'll only lead the way, ladies!"

NINE

Ian stood there, drinking in the sight of her, wondering how it was possible that she had become more sensuous in her pregnancy. Though he tried to control his reaction, he felt the familiar tightness in his groin that the mere sight of her always created. Her mouth was lushly red, and her cheeks had rounded, making her look like a fresh-faced country lass. She wore a thin black stretch velvet tunic and leggings, heightening the white of her skin and the black silk of her hair. The bounty of her breasts drew his eye, as always, and her rounded tummy made him imagine all the ways they could safely make love that he had researched.

Ah, he had missed her!

Tess felt fat and awkward and knew he would see her so. Her face was on fire as his gaze ran over her. Finally, she blurted, "I'll have go back to the States, Ian. You know I will. I can't possibly be locked up like some medieval princess until I give birth, and if I stay with your family, they'll all be targets for the press."

His heart slammed, and his vision blurred for a moment. This, he hadn't expected. Slowly, purposefully, he walked up to her until he towered over her, as close as he could get without touching her burgeoning tummy. He looked down into her sea-blue eyes. "Ye gave me yer solemn promise."

She couldn't bear his expression, for now she knew him well enough to see behind the cool implacability. She saw the pain. "I . . . know, Ian, but we can't pretend it would work for any of us."

"Ye gave me your word."

"Ian," she began, then felt those damned tears start. "I . . ."

But his wide, warm palm was suddenly over her stomach, moving once in a small caress. "I'll not allow ye to leave, lass. Ye promised me." He drew the words out and saw a tear escape to trace her silken cheek. He kept his hand where it was. "I'll issue an edict over the Isle that no one is to help ye leave. I'll cancel all ferries to the mainland. I'll even enlist the aid of Janet and Elsbeth. And . . . I'll sic Kyra on you so I'll know your whereabouts at all times." Now, she knew he was teasing or bluffing. But suddenly he looked startled.

Ah, she realized with a sweet rush, he had felt the babe kick. How she had wanted to share these small wonders with him before! And somehow, he didn't seem repulsed by her girth. On the contrary, she had only to glance down to see the force of his arousal. It made her own breath quicken. But that had nothing to do with the situation at hand. It couldn't.

"Okay, we'll try it." She finally caved in, then finished, "No guarantees, but I'll try. As long as you know that this baby comes first."

"Aye, of a certainty," he said softly, then smiled. "Come, I'll help ye pack."

Life at the castle was much more pleasant than she had anticipated. Aileen had given her a lovely bright suite of rooms and had even had her people turn one of them into a studio for Tess. She awoke that first morning to find her easel already set up, her tarp-covered paintings braced against the wall.

Aileen was the one who knocked on her door as Tess examined the space. When she called, "Come in," it was Aileen who carried the coffee tray.

"Sweet Aileen!" Tess began, stunned. "Oh, I'm . . . I'm sorry." The nickname had slipped out.

"Och," Aileen lapsed into her brogue, " 'tis a family name and one I do love to hear. Lackie bestowed it on me, and his children remember him when they use it." She grinned, somehow looking like an eighteen-year-old coquette. "And aye, 'tis flattering." Then she lifted a determined chin and announced in a slow, deliberate voice, "Whatever happens between you and Ian, my dear, *you and the bairn* will forever be family. Ye must not forget that, Tess." She let her mouth slip into a smile. "I'll bother ye like a sheepdog if ye do. M'children are more than dear to me. And for certain, m'grandchild will always know he is loved."

Tess thought that she had never heard so much of a brogue from her ladyship. A quick bit of a sob slipped out before Tess could stop it. *No.* No time for sentiment. Her baby had to be her first and only concern. The child was all that bound her to the MacLeods anyway.

"You've been talking to Angus," Tess said casually, when she could. "It still might be a girl."

But Aileen only raised a brow, exactly the same way Ian had, and said, "Well, ye know, Tess, Angus predicted the sex, even the characters, of my own children, so I've reason to be swayed by his intuition. But here, now, I've brought ye porridge with raisins and almonds, a bit of milk. It was a favorite of mine when I carried. 'Twill give ye energy for the day." She looked deliberately impartial as she asked, "Did I tell you that Ian arranged your studio himself? He wouldn't allow anyone else to touch your things." Aileen looked down. "But don't worry about changing them about to suit yourself. He didn't even want you to know how possessive he'd been." She looked back over her shoulder from the door. "I wonder why that would be?" And she made her exit, leaving the question hanging in the air.

Kyra took Tess on a tour of the formal gardens. They came across a misting waterfall that was all green and silver, so vivid that it filled the imagination with pictures of unicorns and ancient lairds and their ladies. There, standing among the rich colors and verdant smells of those ferns and trees, she could even imagine the mystical atmosphere of a kind of Camelot.

"I had no idea," Tess whispered in awe. "Here, one can almost believe in fairies and prophecy . . . and intuition. I need to paint."

And paint she did, for hour upon hour. Callie was still Tess's nursemaid, reminding her when she worked too long without a break. But though she let herself become a bit fatigued, she felt she was painting better than she ever had.

Afternoons she had beguiled Ranald into driving her to the side door of the community center so that she could slip in and continue her classes. But she had sworn him to secrecy. They both knew that Ian would never have approved, through he spent little enough time with her and none at all in her bed—which was another little item of interest all its own.

And Michael stayed at Dunvegan. When Michael hadn't stayed in one place since his divorce from her mother, he stayed at sweet Aileen's invitation.

Two weeks into their visit at Castle Dunvegan, he approached her with a certain look in his eye.

"Tess, come and talk to me." He pulled her into the first-floor library and pushed her into a big wingbacked chair. He paced, and she waited. Finally, he put his hands behind his back and turned to face her. "I know I could have given you more attention when you were growing up. You certainly deserved that from me, but . . . well, I was always too worried about making a living for you, your brother, and your mother. It haunted me that I had to be what my own father wasn't. I had to be an adequate provider. What I didn't know was that the more money I made, the more care it would take to keep. Your mother never forgave me." He shook his great head. "Since she died, I haven't quite known . . . where I am. But you have always made me proud, Tess. You are an extraordinary being. I see your talents and gifts shining before me, and I'm proud."

She melted at the extravagance of his praise. "Oh, Pop . . ."

"But, Tess." He sighed. "I worry for you. It's plain to see you're in love with Ian MacLeod. You couldn't hide it if you tried, not from me anyway. So, tell me, what is the difficulty here? Is he what the papers say, an irresponsible womanizer, a man of few interests and little depth?"

Her lower lip trembled a bit as she answered him.

"Oh, no, Pop, you must have had time to see that Ian's not like that at all. There's no difficulty. But . . . you know . . . what Ben and the baby meant to me. I've had my love. All I want now is this child, this miracle child, and to paint what my heart sees. I want peace."

"Forgive me, Tess, I know your grief. We all mourned Ben and the baby with you. But it's been too long. It's time to put it behind you and get on with your life."

"I wish I could, Pop," she answered sadly. "I wish I could."

The reporters had descended on the village. It didn't help that the conflict over the bridge was escalating at the same time. Seeing another story opportunity, the reporters incited both factions, those for and those against the bridge. The stories gave the Skye Bridge national importance as a conservation-versus-economy issue.

Most of the interviews against the bridge were given anonymously, quite probably for fear of reprisals against the damage already done. Angus led those in favor of the bridge and made statements to the mob of reporters, even though he would be forced into early retirement if construction went through. The opposition may have been angered, but, then, who would dare lift a hand against Angus of the Isles?

Ranald grew more and more reluctant to take Tess to the center. He had decided that it was too close to the bed-and-breakfast where the majority of the reporters were staying, and even though none of *them* was allowed to enter the center itself, he feared that too many people knew she was continuing her art classes. It was bound to leak to those sneaking reporters sooner or later, and if they got to Tess, Ian would have his head.

But it was precisely because of the media's relentless pursuit of Tess Hartley, and her affair with the Laird MacLeod, that those against the bridge chose the side entrance of the center to make their stand that afternoon.

Waiting until they knew Tess was inside, Fiona and Jaimie Blair alerted the media and began to orchestrate their demonstration. Jaimie was reckless and headstrong in his beliefs, but for all her posturing, Fiona didn't care a fig for the politics. She was scheming for this publicity to ensure that she enjoyed a satisfying income for a long time to come. If she couldn't have Ian, she could still have the life she wanted.

So, when all were assembled, the Blairs started the crowd chanting and raising their signs for the cameras.

Angus had awakened that morning with a driving impatience so much like anger that it clouded his vision. But he knew there was something he was meant to see. He walked over the green moors in the driving winds until he had something.

Pushing his ancient truck at far too great a speed for the island's narrow, twisting roads, Angus found Ian returning from Kyleakin. Indeed, he nearly ran into him head-on. Angus turned into the turf and was out of the truck in an instant, running with his hobbled gait.

"It is the trouble I feared, Ian!"

Ian knew in that instant that what Angus meant involved Tess. He turned away and whispered her name. Almost immediately, he whirled back to Angus and demanded details, but the old man would only say, "Follow me!" before he hied himself back to his truck and raced over the winding road, Ian following in his car.

By the time they arrived at the center, there appeared to be a full-scale circus in progress.

Angus slammed on his brakes, as did Ian just behind him. He was out of the car and into the heart of the mob before Angus had even opened his own door.

"So." Ian pushed his way through to Jaimie Blair of the upraised fist and sign stating WILL WE WATCH THIS BRIDGE DESTROY OUR SKYE? "At last ye've come into the open, have ye, Blair? And leader of this motley gang, no less? Now that ye've shown your colors, do ye think the people will simply forget the damage ye've already done? D'ye think there will be no hard feelings? Opinions are one thing, but arson, sabotage, vandalism—these crimes of yours have no place here."

"As if ye gave a bloody damn about the Isle and what happens here, Yer Grand Lairdship! What ye're wantin' will be the ruin of us all! There'll be naught here but bloody English investors and condominiums! And a five-pound toll for each trip across. We don't all have your capital at our disposal, but we've a right to protect our way of life here, whether ye like it or no!"

Ian's face grew dark. "The bridge will only make it easier for the merchants as well as the tourists. Even the crofters can take their sheep or their wool to market more easily with that access. We've got to come into the twentieth century, mon, or risk losing all our young people to the opportunities of the cities. There's no reason the council can't put limits on new building." He tossed back his red mane as his eyes narrowed. "Ye pretend to care about the Isle, Blair, but what restitution do yer demonstrators plan for the MacGregor's home and injuries, or the Stuart's shop? Do ye wish a charge of murder brought next, or harm done to yer own?" The laird's power nearly vibrated from him, his conviction was so strong. "It's got to stop, Jaimie, and now! Dear God, think o' yer own mother and sister! What do ye think will happen to them if ye're arrested? D'ye want them to suffer for the things you've done?"

Jaimie flushed a deep red, then spit out, "As if ye

gave a damn about Fiona when ye've had your Yankee whore! Ye must have gotten right at the work for her to be so far along with yer bastard!"

It took less than an instant for Ian to lunge forward, a burning fury behind his eyes. Jaimie lay on the ground, clutching his jaw, when Fiona dropped her sign and went to help her brother to his feet. Both of them glared at Ian. Still the venom spewed from Jaimie. "Did *ye* think about my sister when ye were givin' it to that black-haired American bitch every night?"

Ranald, Geordie, and Davey Ferlow had to hold Ian this time, but Ranald was first to bellow at Jaimie, "No matter that ye're but a lad, Jaimie Blair, and haven't a lick o' sense. Ye'd best be gone from the Isle far and quick as the next ferry or I'll thrash ye m'self when the laird's done w'ye for yer foul mouth an' yer foul deeds! And there are many who'll stand in line behind me for the MacGregors and the harm ye've caused an innocent family! Ye bastard." Ranald shook with rage. "The MacGregor lass is but four years old and would be murdered for yer silly fears!"

That's when the side door opened, and Tess stepped out. Angry, beautiful, and proud, she was also quite obviously close to six months pregnant. The flashbulbs went crazy.

Jaimie shouted above the melee, "Aye, it only needed her, the whore who stole my sister's fiancé! And I'll tell ye that my family is suing the grand

MacLeods for breach of promise!" Jaimie pushed forward again and glared at Ian. "Swallow that, Yer Bloody Lairdship!"

"Jaimie, enough!" Fiona held to her eighteen-year-old brother's arm, but when he tried to break free, he accidently shoved a cameraman, who in turn fell back on another, who then slammed into Tess.

Tess went down, her arms flailing once before she landed hard upon her side with a cry of pain. She lay catching her breath. Ian was there in an instant, cradling her head and shoulders in his arms, his cheek against hers.

"Ah, Tess," he whispered. "Just hold still now. Breathe a wee bit, lass, and then we'll see where we are." He stroked her hair over and over as the mist began to rise.

Jaimie and Fiona had disappeared into the crowd that had become nearly silent save for the flash and click of the cameras. Ian's body shielded Tess for the most part. He concentrated completely on her, dismissing the cameras that cataloged everything, including what they would view as his devotion.

"Tess," Ian was wholly unaware of them as he whispered for her ears only, "I need ye to look at me." Worry forced his heart to pound in his ears as he pulled back enough to see her clearly. When she blinked trustingly, he whispered, "Tell me where it hurts, even a wee bit."

He looked from her widow's peak, down over her

strained brow, and knew she was in pain. When she bit her full lower lip and swallowed hard, he was horribly certain of it. He glanced back over his shoulder, and though he was reluctant to move her, he couldn't simply leave her lying in the drive at the mercy of those cameras.

"All right, love. Hold tight." Ian lifted her quickly and took her inside the center.

She was trembling in reaction, and he held her close while Janet hovered with a blanket and asked a few questions Ian could not hear before she finally murmured about getting Tess "a cuppa." Just at the kitchen door, the iron-haired bit of flurry whirled around and admonished Ian. "Well, sit her down, sit her down, laddie." Then she gave a brisk nod of her head. "We all want the best for our Tess." She choked a bit. "And the bairn. Whate'er we can do will be done."

Ranald had gone around to the side entrance and seemed to be standing sentry with Angus. Only Elsbeth seemed to be missing from Tess's little army of protectors.

"I'm so sorry, Ian," Tess whispered, over and over. "I'm so very sorry for all of this attention on you."

"Dinna fear, sweet, 'tis naught but a bunch of scandalmongers. What do we care for them?" Ian brushed her hair from her brow.

He was sweating. She'd be all right, of course she would.

"You're always saving me." She hiccupped hysterically. Tears flowing, feeling like an idiot, she went on, "But the papers, they'll make you seem uncaring and . . . un . . . un . . . dishonorable."

"Aye. And so?"

"But, you're not, you're not!"

He reached out, and his arms held her tight to his great chest as she shivered. She pulled away to look him in the eye. Now, he thought, she was vulnerable. Now, she would succumb to the least bit of blackmail. But he couldn't do that to his little lass. Tess! Ach, what idiots they were! They both would deny what they most wanted.

But then, did he really know that it was her fear of giving all of herself again that held Tess from him? Perhaps he was misjudging her feelings for him after all.

"I'm fine, Ian." She swallowed again. "I'll be fine." She crooked a finger, beckoning him close enough to whisper in his ear. "I want Hamish. But will you take me to your house, please, or mine, anywhere but the castle . . . not there . . . all that attention." And she closed her eyes as if there was pain. She took a breath. "If anything bad happens, it has to be between us. Please. I couldn't bear to see their faces if . . . if . . ."

Ian sighed heavily, feeling as if an anvil suddenly pressed down on his chest. He murmured, "I'm taking ye to hospital, dearling. I'll have a helicopter here in a half hour, I promise."

Tess took a chance then. She reached up to cup his cheeks so that he had no choice but to look into her eyes.

"I want Hamish."

Then his own eyes narrowed as he realized there was a reason, an agenda here. "Ye're trying to keep the publicity to a minimum?" he asked, knowing it was true. "Ye've never lied to me before, Tess. Dinna do so now."

At last she gave a sober nod. "But I'll go to the mainland if you don't trust Hamish completely. I'll go to Glasgow or London if you think it will make a difference. Ian," she said slowly, "I want this baby, more than you could ever imagine. I don't believe I'm anything but a little bruised. My stomach was clenching, but I think it was only panic. Hamish can check the baby's heartbeat and tell us right away if I need more attention. Please, Ian . . . all the publicity—I don't want it for you or for Michael."

Ian nodded and brushed her cheek before he gave instructions to Ranald in a hoarse voice. The helicopter would be waiting for them, just in case. Outside, a twenty-foot gauntlet of reporters stood between the center and Ian's car. Angus ran interference, and Ian carried Tess through them as if they didn't even exist.

TEN

Her face pressed to his warm neck, all Tess could think about was what she had done to Ian, and how much he truly hated such publicity.

Then the volley of questions from the reporters began; "Are you planning to marry Lord MacLeod, Tess? Has he asked you? Will you be taking the baby back to the States with you, or do you think the laird's family will sue for custody while you're in Great Britain?"

That one question struck through all the others, and Tess felt the color drain from her face. Before she had a chance to answer it, others overlapped. "When is the baby due? Is it really Lord MacLeod's child? Is it true that you broke up the laird's engagement? Will you sign a prenuptial agreement?"

"No comment!" With Ranald's help Ian pushed his way through the crowd to his car. "No bloody comment!" He finally had her inside his car and locked the door before shoving his way to the other side and sliding behind the wheel.

When Tess looked out the window, she saw Janet batting at reporters with a rolled newspaper as if they were naughty puppies and almost wanted to laugh. What she really wanted to do was cry, but she wouldn't give in to the impulse. Calm, she must stay calm.

Ian spoke to her in a soothing voice as he drove the mile to his house. "Okay, m'lass." One arm came around her to give her a reassuring squeeze before it returned to the shift. He forced a sense of calm into his voice. "Tell me what ye're feeling. Is there pain— what kind?"

"I *won't* lose this baby, Ian! I won't! Do you hear me?" Tess sat with her fists clenched in her lap. "Don't even think it!"

"Here, love," he said when he wanted only to fold her into his arms. "Everything will be all right." He went on in the calmest voice he could summon. "Pull it together now. Tell me exactly, have ye pain or cramping?"

She tilted her head and shook it, then said, "A little." They were almost at the manor house. Hamish and the helicopter would be there as soon as they were contacted.

Tess dragged in a breath. "Some," she corrected. Then she hiccuped a sob. "Oh, Ian, what if . . . if . . .?"

Ian's eyes were dark green. "Listen to me, Tess. Ye stop worrying now. Ye're not alone, and it'll only hurt the bairn. Just suspend yer thoughts. Can ye do that for me? Can ye try?"

Tess bit her lip. "Yes."

"There's m'lass." Looking into her eyes, he drew a smile from her, as he always could. A moment later he pulled into the drive of the manor house and stopped the car before he bent to give her a gentle sweetheart's kiss. He carried her inside, her heart pounding against his all the while.

Ian put her into one of his mother's nightgowns with the same care he'd have given a two-year-old babe and sat beside the bed, her hand in his, as he whispered that she should close her eyes. Then he waited, head down.

He didn't even know he was praying.

Elsbeth arrived. She pushed Ian from the room and let her hands rove Tess's belly as she proceeded to reassure the young woman in her own dear, bullying way that she had assisted hundreds of mothers to healthy childbirth. She raised a sparse gray brow and announced that any number of them had fallen at one time or another during their pregnancy, but it was most dangerous very early in their term, and Tess was months past that vulnerable time. That was her most reassuring information.

The verdict they waited for came thirty minutes later when Hamish arrived. Tess was to stay in bed for a couple of days, to be certain. But everything seemed to be quite all right with the bairn.

That night, while Tess showered, Ian made up a pallet next to her bed. When she came into the room, he was standing at the window in silhouette, a great dark shadow with a glass of brandy in his hand. He heard her behind him, frowned down into his glass, and announced, "Dinna tell me to go, Tess, for I willna do it. Here I am, and here I stay. Ye need my care as much as I need to know that ye have someone close at hand to aid ye."

"All right," Tess said softly, smiling as she wondered at herself. Whenever in her life had she been so compliant?

"All right?" Ian's deep voice seemed harsh. He couldn't quite believe it either.

"Yes, all right!" She bit her soft bottom lip. She had decided she was going to gamble. She might as well gamble big. "But I'd rather have you here, holding me. That is, if . . . you wouldn't mind."

"Ach, Tess, my Tess," Ian sighed as he came and gathered her into his arms. "Wherever did ye learn so many ways to disconcert a man?"

They lay entwined, arms and legs, with her head on his shoulder as the darkness helped neither of them to sleep.

"I've let myself become so involved with your family, Ian," Tess finally whispered one of the fears that preyed upon her mind in the night.

"I can't help but wonder, what if something happens?"

"Have ye no value on yer own then?" Ian sat up against the headboard, pulling her with him. "Apart from what ye are to me, ye are a person to be reckoned with, Tess, and ye've made all here know it well! Look at yer center and the way it's changed Dunvegan! Look at the winter prosperity, the self-esteem you've brought the people!" He let that sink in before he continued, "As for our son, he lies snug and healthy." His hand caressed her round tummy in a slow circling motion. "Still feisty." He chuckled, pressing the place that gave his hand a swift kick. "So, now, will ye finally be done with yer daft talk?" He gathered her closer. "Aye, it's been a harrowing day, but we're past it." He tilted his head down toward her and asked, now stroking the soft skin of her inner arm, "Fine now, dearling?"

She nodded, then gulped and nodded once more. "Ian."

"Aye, love."

Funny, she thought, how quickly she had become used to his endearments. "If . . . if there's no harm to the baby, and in a few days Hamish says it's okay, would you still want to marry me?"

He breathed. Air in. Air out. Then he had to remember to breathe again at all. He knew she offered only out of a sense of obligation, but he would take her on those terms. The time had come.

"Aye," he said low, as he smiled down into her eyes.

"After all," she confided, a few minutes, a few sweet kisses later, "I think you're right about it being the best solution. And as you said, we can always divorce after the baby's born."

"Oh, aye," he said quickly, without a touch of emotion. *Like bloody hell they would!* was what he was thinking as he settled her comfortably against him.

Tess smiled back and sighed, then placed another quick kiss on her lover's perfect mouth. "If it's a boy, I want to name him after you, then my father. But if, just if, Angus is wrong, and it's a girl, I'd like to call her Aileen Marie," She murmured between nibbles and brushes against those wicked, smiling lips.

His cheeks flushed with pleasure. She felt them heat.

What was this she was feeling, she wondered? Pregnancy hormones? Simple relief? In the end she didn't care what was causing this warm tide of emotion. It made her feel connected to this beautiful man, and it was lovely.

"Ye know," Ian said, his smile quirking at the thought, "there are bound to be fierce bouts with Aileen over the spoiling of the bairn."

"I think I'm up to it," Tess responded cockily.

Ian studied her from head to toe in his own slow, sensuous fashion. "Aye, ye just might be, at that."

They held each other for another while before

she finally asked, "Ian, would you tell me about your father?"

"What?" Ian was jolted. That was certainly an unexpected question, and he felt his palms grow clammy in response.

She had felt his body tense, but that didn't stop her. "Your mother said you almost died trying to save him."

There was only silence.

"Was he a good man? Was he kind?" she probed, thinking it was a subject that needed probing.

"Why d'ye care?" he asked irritably. But his arms only tightened around her.

"Because our child will inherit something of him . . . and your mother sees so much of him in you. And as soon as I think I know you a little, I'm surprised again."

Ian's arms tightened even more. His voice was husky as he said, "You know me, everything worth the knowing."

"Perhaps I wish to know those things you think are not worth knowing." She kissed his chest, finding a hard pebble there to nuzzle with the tip of her nose before she drank in the rich scent of him. "And you'd better humor me if you want me for your wife, your Lairdship," she whispered as she looked up into his fathomless eyes. "Because it's a borderline case."

He let the shadow of a smile steal back across his

lips and asked outright, "Ye're saying there's a bit of blackmail involved?"

Her smile was whimsical. "Perhaps." Then she waited.

At last he spoke in a slow, solemn voice. "He was a big man. Good with his hands." He smiled a half-smile. "He wasn't one for idle conversation. But he and sweet Aileen didn't need many words. They would simply look at each other." His eyes showed something he felt at the memory, and she reached out to him. He sighed. "Da's voice was a low rumble. I don't remember it ever being raised in anger. But he would give ye a look, his voice would get slow and clipped. Then ye knew ye were in trouble. The last thing ye ever wanted was to disappoint him." Ian stared at a window for a moment before he cleared his throat. "Ye knew that every word he spoke was the absolute truth. All of us were certain he was invincible."

They held hands for a few minutes until his strong fingers tightened so much that she gave a small gasp of pain. He loosened his grip with a murmur and kissed her fingers in apology.

"What happened?" she asked, sure he'd been thinking of the day his father died.

"What happened?" Ian looked at her with a veiled expression. "He had taken me sailing. It was summer, and one of the few times I had him all to myself. My brother and sister were both visiting friends in Edinburgh with Aileen. He allowed me to captain for the first time, and I thought my heart would burst with pride. We had gone out farther than we should, but the wind was so right, neither of us noticed." He swallowed hard, and her other hand brushed his rough cheek. He wouldn't look at her. "Then there was a sudden, unexpected squall."

She'd never seen a look like that on his face. "You don't have to say any more, Ian," Tess hurried to tell him.

His breath huffed out. "One great wave came over us and broke the mast, fouling the lines. We were both caught, but Da was thrown over the side, while I was trapped aboard until I found some broken glass on deck and finally cut my way free."

His beautiful mouth tightened, and she whispered in horror, "Oh, Ian."

"I dived for him . . . until I had no wind left. My hands and feet were so numb, I couldn't— It wasn't enough."

Tess stared. So this was what he carried behind those cool green eyes. She lifted a hand to his bleak face and let her thumb brush away the drop of moisture that had slipped over his cheek.

"It was everything, Ian, every single heroic thing that you could do." She gave a little sob and kissed him in sweet benediction. "I thank God you're here, and safe." Her cheek rubbed over his, their tears mingling.

Ian gave a low groan and pulled her to him as if he

might absorb her into his own body. Dear heaven, he couldn't have said when it had happened, or how, but he loved Tess as he'd never thought to love a woman in this life.

ELEVEN

They were married on the Isle because Ian refused to let Tess travel as far as Edinburgh. He also thought there would be fewer reporters still on the Isle than they would be exposed to in the city.

Her dress was an off-the-shoulder classic design in cream-colored lace with seed pearls hastily put together by Elsbeth and her class. If she was going to resemble a barge, at least it would be a beautiful vessel.

Baroque pearl earrings were Michael's gift. There had been a surprise bridal shower held at the center. Janet lent her grandmother's pearl bracelet. Aileen gave Tess a warm hug and the veil her own mother had handed down.

"I've never seen Ian so content," she whispered. "And I can hardly wait to start spoiling my grandson."

Tess grinned. "Ian's already warned me of the danger." And they laughed.

Kyra presented her with an embroidered blue satin garter. Well, "presented" might be not be the best word. Actually, Kyra shot her with it from between two fingers with one green eye closed.

It had been a lovely party.

For the wedding Tess wore the diamond-studded thistle, and Michael gave her away while Kyra stood as bridesmaid. A red-faced Ranald was shocked to find himself best man, and Janet and Elsbeth cried in tandem. Aileen glowed her own approval as the vows were said. Even Angus was there.

Leaving the kirk, they faced a few reporters, but within minutes they were on their own. There was no reception. Ian wanted no other targets for the press. He had kept their destination a secret, although he told her they would stay on the Isle. He put Tess into the Saab as if she were crystal. She still had difficulty in cars, but she wanted to hide the problem from Ian as much as possible. He had enough to cope with apart from her leftover paranoia.

Within twenty minutes he pulled up to a two-story, ivy-covered cottage.

"It's one of the MacDonald weekend cottages, and the last place anyone will look for us," he told her, helping her out of the car, then waiting for her reaction.

She looked it over, from the smoking stone chimney, the lead-paned windows, down to the great carved oak door. The walk was made of a curving design in flagstone, and a rich green lawn rose on either side of it. A wild stream Ian called a "burn" slipped over black rocks and flowed under a tiny bridge.

"Oh, Ian." She smiled, grateful for his thoughtfulness. "It's perfect! I couldn't wish for a more beautiful honeymoon cottage."

Ian grinned. "The best part is that Callie has come and gone, and we will be"—the look he gave her then set her pulse racing in a wonderfully familiar way—"absolutely . . . completely . . . splendidly . . . alone."

She reached up with one arm and pulled him down for a warm kiss. "I'm so happy," she whispered into his ear before she gave the lobe a little bite. "Now, you get to carry me over the threshold." She laughed. "I hope Your Lairdship is up to it."

Fiona Blair slammed the letter she had received from her lawyer on top of the paper with the picture of Tess and Ian leaving the kirk in Portree on the front page. She pounded them both with her fist until there was no more feeling.

Whirling around, she screamed, "Jaimie!"

❧━━━━━━━━━━━━━❧

Smiling at the scene she had set, Tess carefully lit the candelabra she had snitched from the dining room and put Mozart on the bedroom CD player. The frothy bubbles were almost to the rim when she turned the faucets and let her robe slide down her arms to the floor.

Her eyelids half-closed as she sank down until her head rested against a hand towel she had placed at one end of the ancient porcelain tub. She began to lather her perfumed soap with a fat sea sponge. She lay back with a soft groan of pleasure, letting her thoughts float.

She had dreamed of him the night before last, a wildly erotic dream that had left her aching. She woke late that morning, and when she had come into the kitchen, there he stood. She could hardly face him, stammering and blushing over nothing. Ian had given her a few questioning glances and finally asked how she was feeling.

"Good . . . I mean, fine . . . Why?" She bit her full bottom lip and pulled at the high neckline of the oversized sweater she wore.

She didn't know how her self-consciousness had charmed him, or how much he needed her and her lushly sweet red mouth.

Again. Still. More.

He smiled in a way that was completely male, for

her voluptuous beauty still astounded him. "Ye are bonnie, lass."

Tess gave a shake of her head, looked at Callie's back at the stove, then blushed apricot. "I wasn't fishing," she said quickly. "I mean, I don't need compliments."

"We know well what fishing is in Scotland, lass," Ian announced with great forbearance, his green eyes teasing her. "And it's possible ye might yet enjoy a compliment."

Her own eyes had admonished him furiously, but he had simply appealed to the gaunt woman by the stove. "Should a man not tell his lass she's a beauty, Callie *mor*? Should he not tell her what the sight of her does to him?"

Callie actually giggled, though Tess had never heard her do so before and was surprised to hear it now. Then the woman who rarely volunteered more than "Aye" or "Nay" announced decidedly, "Y'know, laddie, some girls demand a slower pace of a mon than others."

That had left both of them staring at the back of Callie's head before their eyes met, shocked into camaraderie, and Ian answered with a half-quirked smile, "I'll do my best to remember that, Callie *mor*." His eyes gleamed as he watched the blush rise to her cheeks.

Now, in her warm bath, Tess lifted her sponge, squeezing the silky water over one shoulder, then the other, as she shook her head. The pull of the man was getting more and more difficult to resist. He seemed to have become her lodestone, and her weakness.

Suddenly, Tess heard the quick knock and the creak of her bedroom door before she saw Ian standing in the open doorway of the bathroom.

"Ah, God!" he breathed out desperately, and shook his head in wonder. "Ah, Tess." He groaned. She glanced up and froze to see him there, staring at her with a fierce hunger she knew he saw in her own eyes.

She didn't raise her hands to cover herself. She had to be sure. She had to see him, then glance casually down his body to reassure herself of her effect on him.

When he grew to great proportions quite visibly beneath her gaze, she couldn't help the feminine smile that came and went so quickly. He wasn't even certain he'd seen it. She looked up at him, and her eyes seemed huge and full of promise as her hands gripped the sides of the ancient tub.

"It would seem ye have need of someone to scrub yer back." Tess saw the gleam in his eyes as his heavy lids lowered.

"Perhaps, if that someone wouldn't be offended at my size."

"Quite the contrary, this . . . sweet shape o' yours is a special attraction. Full of child. Rich with life, our life," he whispered, each word a dramatic pronouncement.

Her eyelids lowered. Dear heaven, but the man knew women and romance. He seemed to love saying things like "with child" or "carrying."

"Are you conning me, Ian?" she finally demanded point-blank. Tess took a deep breath and waited, thinking how American she was, while he was so British . . . or Scots . . . but foreign, and quite proper, all the same.

What might have been a bitter expression crossed Ian's face, and his chin lifted proudly. "Ye have the need to ask me that?"

Her eyes filled again with the tears she seemed to be powerless to withhold. "Of course I do, you idiot man! Look at me!"

Then he came to her and dropped dramatically to one knee before he took her face in both hands. "Ye are lovely to me. And if ye have new curves, they come from yer body nurturing my son. Ye cannot ken what that means to a man, Tess. But if it was the bairn of another, if it was Ben's, ye would still be bonnie to me. For ye are the woman I love."

She flooded him with tears, and he held her, never minding the wet. In comfort he kissed her, meaning it to be brief, but the hunger flared, and soon they were both wild with need.

Ian drew breath and pulled back, smiling a teasing smile as he took up the bath sponge and fragrant soap she used. The look in his eyes fueled her hunger. He washed her, murmuring that he well remembered the first time he had bathed her, when she was ill.

"Your beautiful body was a terrible test for my restraint. I wanted you every moment." His voice played along her senses. "I'm finding myself even more affected now, dearling." He drew her to her feet and dried her with a huge towel before he lifted her in his arms and carried her to the bed. There, he sat on the edge, cuddling her in his lap with a reverence she found dear. As always, she was overwhelmed by the size of the man, his strength and his contrasting gentleness with her. Her hand found one rough cheek, drawing him close for her kiss. Quickly, she began to tremble. It had been too long.

"Ah, love," he murmured, moving his warm, enticing kisses down her neck. She could feel his arousal beneath her, pushing against the tight material of his trousers. She turned a kiss into his soft hair, and he groaned.

When he pulled back, he looked steadily into her eyes as he rubbed the intricate carving of the wedding band he had placed upon her hand that afternoon. He raised it to his lips for a kiss and placed it gently in her lap. Then he slid one finger from her collarbone to the deep line of her cleavage, loosening the towel until it fell to either side of her body, and she was open to him. Her breasts swelled; her stomach clenched. Even her toes were curling.

His scalding mouth found her breast. Around and around, his kisses circled. She arched up against him, dying for that heat to reach her swollen, aching nipple.

Finally, he drew her into his mouth and sucked with such force that she cried out at the lightning connection to her womb. Suddenly, he was gone, and she was left gasping!

"Did I hurt ye, lassie?" His voice was hoarse and anxious.

"Come back," she commanded urgently, then softened. "Please."

Ian's smile was tender as he bent to obey. He made an art of it, teasing one swollen breast, then the other. His hand slid up behind her knee and caressed the sensitive silken flesh there. Finally, he turned them so that she lay on the bed, and he kissed and licked her belly. Running his hands over its sweet roundness, he seemed unable to get his fill.

Staring into her eyes, he pulled back long enough to bend her knees, bracing her feet on the mattress so that her pink flesh was completely open to him. Tess blushed deeply when she saw him examining her. She felt her own damp heat and closed her eyes when he let his thumb brush over that most sensitive fold of moist flesh. He parted her, stroking her first lightly, then provocatively, as he touched her everywhere.

She was panting now, deep in his spell. She felt his fingers glide more easily as her arousal grew. But when she reached up to grab his arms and pull him to her, he drew back.

"No," he whispered huskily, "let me . . ." He pushed her arms back down to her sides and murmured, "Don't move." He slipped away to the bathroom and returned almost immediately, a bottle of pale oil in his hands. He placed it on the bedside table and stood up to undress in the firelight.

Tess sighed softly at the sight of his broad muscled chest covered in crisp cotton. His hands went to his belt buckle, and she whispered, "Hurry."

He grinned as he had a thought. "No, I don't think so." His eyes went to her breasts, and he felt the blood pounding in his groin and temples. When her hand moved self-consciously to her stomach, he groaned. "Do ye no' ken that the sight of ye like this is so erotic, I'm fairly coming out o' my skin?"

Tess gulped and took a deep breath. Ian reached for the bottle of oil. He smiled at her as he poured a bit into his hand and placed the bottle back on the bedside table. He rubbed his hands together and then put a knee upon the edge of the bed before he slid his hands over her shoulders, her arms, and up in languid motions. At last he let them glide to her full breasts.

Ah, she was delicious! He took his time, massaging the delicate, translucent skin, making each nerve ending sizzle with a life of its own.

The rich, erotic scent of almonds filled her nostrils, and her knees began to slide down until Ian stopped them. His eyes met hers with warm promise. Then he proceeded to smooth even more oil over her rounded belly, pausing momentarily as he felt what he thought must be a tiny foot or a pointed elbow. He smiled down at her in a way that made her heart beat even faster than it did before. It was a look of possession and care.

When he reached again for the oil, he told her, "Turn on yer side now, wife. That way." He pointed away from him.

She suppressed a shiver of sensation and looked up at him with questions in her eyes that Ian soon answered.

"I read a bit," he said, though the truth was that he had devoured every treatise on pregnancy he could get in his hands. He oiled his palms again and gave her a lazy grin. "I had an idea ye might fancy a back rub."

She felt oddly vulnerable with her back to him until the first familiar warmth of his touch. He began a thorough, expert massage on the muscles of her shoulders and middle and lower back. His hands were both strong and sensitive. Where Tess had first been aroused by Ian's touch, this kind of pleasure relief was different and diverted her senses.

"Oh, Ian." She sighed. "That feels so wonderful . . . ah!" For weeks she had had an almost constant pain in her lower back. It was quite normal, Elsbeth had reassured her, but it was lovely to have her aches catered to by the wild and gentle Laird MacLeod.

She was nearly asleep as he began working on her hips and the sweet curves of her bottom with a difference in his touch that was just barely discernible. The sexual being awoke again at his rhythmic stroking. He kneaded the muscles of her hips, then slowed as he worked his way downward until she squirmed and moaned in helpless pleasure. At last she turned over on her back in one swift move and reached for Ian's wide shoulders.

Looking up into his eyes, she whispered hoarsely, "I've missed you so much!"

He gathered her close and rocked her as he murmured into her ear, "Never as much as I've missed ye, love!" He breathed warm gusts of air into the soft strands of dark hair, and the delicate scent of it came back to tease him. "Are ye . . . do you think . . . ?"

"Yes," she interrupted in a fever of impatience, her hands running over his shoulders and down his thickly muscled arms. "Oh, yes!" She felt the quiver that ran through him echo in her own body and turned her mouth to his. "Ian," she whispered eagerly.

"Aye, lass." His fingers sifted through her silky hair and crushed it in his fists.

Her blood rushed through her veins in a frantic race to pool in her womb, between her thighs, in her breasts and tingling fingertips. Whimpering with impatience, she dragged her fingers recklessly over the buttons of his shirt until her skin touched his. She had to feel him, the skin and muscle and bones that held him together. She shifted one way, then the other, hot skin to hot skin and the rough curls that covered his wide chest. She threw her head back with a ragged breath as her hands tugged the shirt down his arms.

When his shirt caught at the wrists, Ian tore his way free. Once released, his arms went round her to move her body against his in one long, sinuous motion. As he kneaded her back and hips, his breath came fast and hard. His temples pounded, and the burning ache in his groin became nearly unbearable.

His hand found the soft nest of curls between her legs. She was hot and moist and moved with each motion of his fingers. Her own hands had fallen to his belt and, as if too tempted, slipped down to his hard shape in a butterfly caress before she opened his belt, then his trousers.

"Stand up," she whispered, then grinned. "And help me sit up."

He grinned back and performed as ordered. His reward was the feel of her hands upon him once more. Sliding trousers and briefs to the floor, she lifted her gaze as her hands rose to warm his sleek, muscular hips. His arousal pulsed in the thick thatch of dark red curls, and she caught her breath.

"Och, but ye're a beautiful laddie buck," she teased him with something of a smile. Then she laughed at his blush. "I didn't know you could still do that."

Ian raised a brow. He knew exactly what she was laughing at. And he knew exactly how to draw her attention back to the more important issues. One simple, low-voiced command. "Lie back." And he took control once again.

He looked down at her, her white skin glistening with oil, and closed his eyes for a moment as he anticipated the slide of her skin against his when he surged into her. God! It had been so long!

She shivered when she saw the tightening of his features. "Ian," she whispered. "Come to me!"

Her eager demand was as exciting as a lush caress, and he was beside her in an instant, one arm sliding behind her knees and lifting them as he positioned himself.

"Spread your knees a bit, love," he said raspily, now as impatient as she. When she obeyed, he reached down to her moist entrance and caressed her until she gave a soft gasp of surrender. He lifted his hips to fill her with his throbbing warmth. Her own wet heat seared him, and he groaned, flexing, rotating his hips as he seated himself completely. Tess choked back a sob, and he began a lavish rhythm that made her moan in helpless pleasure. He waited until she was close to the edge before he withdrew to pull her astride his hard thighs.

Her eyes were dazed, but her limbs moved each

way he placed her. And soon she found herself sliding down onto his shaft, his hands at her hips, her thighs clenching with pleasure.

"I couldn't see your face." He panted, his hands brushing her taut nipples and opulent breasts. "I wanted to see your face." His look scorched her, and his fingers grazed the sensitive bud of flesh between her legs, circling round and round.

"Ian . . ."

His hips lifted her like an untamed pony, and she ground down to further the exquisite penetration. He let her set the pace until she drove him so high, he feared he might finish without her.

She threw her head back, tossing her beautiful hair over her shoulders. Her lips were parted, eyes closed. Ian smiled and rocked her once, then again, before her world exploded into wild, ecstatic sensation. She screamed without ever knowing she had made a sound. And when he came inside her, he shuddered with emotion.

TWELVE

They had two weeks in that lovely cottage and became closer than Tess had imagined possible. Their second night, Tess had waited until Ian was out back, replenishing the coal bin, then struggled to pull his portrait, finally completed, from the trunk of the Saab.

He must have heard something, because he was behind her as soon as she slammed the trunk closed. Taking the unwieldy, framed canvas, he scolded her for trying to lift something so heavy. Once inside, he leaned it against the mantel and helped her off with her coat. Tess ducked her head shyly and settled into one of the fat armchairs before the fire.

"It's for you," she said, plucking nervously at the brocade.

Sensing the importance of this gift, Ian smiled as he walked to the mantel and turned the canvas. Then he backed slowly to her chair and perched on one of its arms beside her. He stared at the painting for a long time before he covered her hand with his warm palm and whispered, "Thank you, wife." Her hand turned over in his, and their fingers laced.

That same night, Ian presented Tess with his own wedding present, an emerald necklace with matching earrings in an antique gold setting.

She sighed in wonder. "They're the color of your eyes."

"Then ye'll remember me," he said.

"Aye," she answered with a soft laugh.

Supplies, baked goods, even flowers, were left outside the door by Callie every other day. Tess and Ian cooked together, cleaned together. To her amused surprise Tess found that her pampered laird was no stranger to a kitchen but an accomplished "plain" cook and a very efficient scullery helper.

Much of their time was spent in bed, exploring pleasure during pregnancy, but Ian also took her on long rambling walks about the countryside. They chuckled over the antics of the early lambs. Ian taught her to fish and got slapped in the head with her first catch as she yanked it from the water. They laughed so hard at the accident that the fish slipped its hook, and, still laughing, they decided to reward its heroic efforts by setting it free.

Evenings, they sat before the fire playing Scrabble or listening to the stereo. Ian taught Tess the reel and a few other traditional dances. She taught him the two-step and some Cajun dance moves. Some nights Ian played piano while Tess sketched. And they slept every night entwined, loving, sharing.

It was glorious.

When they returned to the manor house at last, they were bound together by the ties of those intimacies. And even though they resumed their own schedules, one was never far from the other's thoughts.

The last month of her pregnancy, Tess finally slowed down. She was terribly uncomfortable, and there wasn't much she could do. The pressure was so great on her kidneys that she made certain she was always within dashing distance of the bathroom.

Ian rubbed her back every night and catered to her moods and whims. And when she burst into tears of frustration at her helplessness to control herself, he held her close and sang Scottish love songs to her.

"How can you stand it?" she demanded one night. "I hate the way I've been acting!"

"Ye're overburdened, is all, m'lass." He stroked her silky dark hair away from her face. "And if ye can put up with all that ye have for the sake of our bairn, I can force a bit of patience for yer witch's temper."

"Devil!" She pulled away to punch him in one strong arm.

"M'lady." He nodded mockingly, knowing it would make her laugh.

It did, before she ordered, "Lie down."

"Tess?" One auburn brow rose. "Ye're too far gone, love, for games of the kind you're thinking."

"Aye, perhaps." She grinned as she pressed his shoulders back. "But you've always been an inventive lad."

Her labor started not long after they fell asleep that night and continued for the next eighteen hours. Waiting for the helicopter, coordinating the arrival of both Hamish and Elsbeth, Ian found the first of those hours the longest. When they were finally at the hospital, they were separated while Tess was prepped. Then the test of her endurance began. At one point Hamish nearly decided to do a cesarian. But she demanded that he wait until the last possible second before he did so.

Ian knelt beside her with tears that never made it past his lashes as he went through the pain of each contraction with her. "There's m'lass," he chanted. "That's it, here you go. Here's the peak . . . and now . . . it's passed." His own breath would sigh out then. "Aye, that's fine. Our laddie's almost here. Ye're doing fine."

———————

Michael had been called back from Switzerland, and Kyra had been waiting with Aileen at the Edinburgh residence for a week. So the troops were all assembled when Ian came into the waiting room with a wide grin.

"Ian Michael Lachlan MacLeod has just taken the world quite by storm! The staff has already nicknamed him Lackie." He nodded to Michael. "No offense, sir, but I'm afraid all our own plans are for naught. It fits the little heathen too well." A small sound came from Aileen, and Michael put his arm around her.

"Well, someone bloody congratulate me! I'm a father!"

They all surged forward.

"Tess is all right?" Kyra asked first.

"Fine," he answered as he brushed his sister's cheek. "She's resting. Ah, but Kie, ye should have seen her face in that first moment she held Lackie. I'll never forget the sight!"

He was beautiful, so new, a miracle of life. Lackie. Every day brought a fresh surprise, a new accomplishment. Tess knew she was lost in the wonder of it, and she had no shame.

Ian was equally enthralled by the tiny being who

was his son. It was he who sang the lullabies of moons and stars and the fairies of the isles. And when he watched Tess suckle Lackie in his grandmother's rocker, he photographed the moment in his mind to pull out when he was old and gray.

If life at home was peaceful, island politics were not. A British investor visiting in Portree had been mugged and beaten by two men with blackened faces, a kind of crime unheard of on Skye. Alisdair Clark, another visitor, who had come to the Isle to speak at a gathering about the economic benefits of the bridge, was run off the road in Glendale. He was left with a concussion and a broken arm. One of the bed-and-breakfasts in Dunvegan was broken into and vandalized. More serious, the Blair cottage was burned to the ground.

The council voted to hire more people to patrol both roads and towns in pairs. Men and women, some even volunteers, were armed with no more than billy clubs and radios. The pubs were asked to close early, and everything was locked up tight by midnight. People were getting frightened.

The evening before the final council meeting on the bridge, Angus appeared at the door of the manor house.

"Hello, Angus." Tess smiled her welcome. "Did you know Duke has a special bark for you alone? You're just in time for Callie's roast beef. Come in, come in."

"How fares the bairn?" Angus brushed the damp from his feet and stepped into the house, patting the dog that jumped at his side.

She laughed with maternal pride. "Fat, demanding, and looking more like his father every day. Seven weeks, and he looks like a three-month-old." She poured Angus his usual whisky. "Would you like to see him?"

"Ta, lass." He took the glass and bobbed his head. "But perhaps I could have a word with Ian before I go up."

"Oh, no," she stated, with wifely arrogance. "Ian's had enough meals ruined with all the trouble in the last few days. You'll have dinner with us, then you two can talk. Lackie will wait."

"Aye, lass." Angus bowed to the lady of the house.

Tess turned away to hide her grin. Perhaps there was something to this stuffy Old World courtesy after all.

Later, Ian took Angus to his study. No sooner was the door closed behind him than Angus spoke.

"Jaimie Blair never left the Isle, nor Fiona either. They've been staying with MacDonald cousins, having meetings and plotting trouble."

Ian frowned. "Does Gordon MacDonald know of this?"

"Nay." Angus shook his gray head. "Ye know he's for the bridge. The old crust would never countenance violence in any case. He's too much the parliamentarian. 'Twas one of the MacDonalds, young Chris, who came to me."

"D'ye think they're still there? We've enough evidence against James Blair now to prosecute."

"The house is deserted. We drove by. But Chris told me of a place they might have made for, the abandoned kirk in Uig. Another thing, they've our radio frequency."

Ian absorbed that. "Will Chris testify?"

"Aye. I've tucked him away with his uncle Gordon for that purpose." Angus lit his pipe, and the two men smiled in satisfaction.

"Well, now." Ian went to the window and lifted the drapes to look out, into the darkness and the mist. "I've some phone calls to make. We'll see if we can arrange for a few friends to meet us along the way."

Angus never did make it upstairs to see Lackie. He and Ian spoke to Ranald, but Ian told Tess only that they were going out to speak to some of the dissidents.

"Don't wait up for me, love." He hugged her good-bye with one arm about her shoulders. "You know how these things go. Each side talks until the other's too tired to argue anymore. You get a good sleep and don't ask questions when ye feel the warm body join ye in the night."

"Mmm." She strengthened her hold on him. "You mean there might be a surprise finish to these long weeks without you?"

He dragged her behind the kitchen door and sucked lightly on her soft neck, showing off his ready passion for her. "Did Hamish really give ye the go-ahead?"

"He did indeed." She grabbed both of his firm buns and squeezed. "So talk fast tonight, and I might let you wake me."

"Bloody hell," he murmured, giving her a warm smack on the lips. Then he grinned. "Now I'll be hard as a rock all night." He turned and walked out of the kitchen muttering, "I'll pay ye back later."

"Don't pick any fights, Ian. And let Duke out when you go," she called after him. "I'll let him in when I'm ready for bed." Ian raised a hand in acknowledgment. Then they were gone.

Tess gave Lackie his ten o'clock feeding and couldn't wait up anymore. Her eyes felt as if they were weighted with lead. Looking out the kitchen window as she locked up, she saw the lights from Ranald's cottage in the back and was reassured, as always, by his presence. She thought it strange that Duke didn't come when she called for him but decided that Ian could let him in when he got home. With a last flip of the lock she stretched high and turned toward the stairs.

A quick shower and she was in bed in less than ten minutes, asleep in three more. But she wasn't long asleep when it happened.

There was a small noise on the baby intercom, and she woke with a mother's instinct. But when she opened her eyes, she only had time to see some dark material coming down over her. The next moment she felt the smothering of a rough blanket and called out in protest. Her hands were bound to her sides, and she felt something like a rope going round and round her body. She knew immediately that her struggles were useless, but she couldn't help it.

"Lackie," she screamed. "Lackie!" Understanding of what was happening swept through her, and she cried out in a panic, "Don't hurt my baby—please, don't hurt my baby!"

Suddenly, she felt herself lifted into the air and carried across the room. She realized they had stopped before the closet. She heard the squeak of the door, and then she was dropped unceremoniously to the floor. The door slammed and locked behind her. The click of the key echoed in her ears, and she whispered desperately, "Ian!"

Fifteen minutes later Tess had squirmed and twisted her torso free. That was all she needed. The closet doors were double, with a single key lock on the knob. It didn't take much more force than the weight of her body to crash through them.

Gasping with desperation, she stumbled back to her feet and ran for the door of the nursery. "No!" she cried out when she saw the empty crib. Her fingernails dug into the paint of the doorframe as she screamed,

"No!" and fell to her knees, sobbing. Then, sobbing at the same time she dragged in great gulps of air, she staggered to her feet and ran for the telephone.

The line had been cut.

Her next thought was for Ranald. They must have done something to him! Tears pouring with every step, she threw open the back door and ran for his small cottage.

She found him sprawled inside the door. His head was bleeding, and he was unconscious. But as soon as she felt his limbs for broken bones, he moaned and began to come to. He tensed, beginning to struggle, then he recognized her voice saying, "It's Tess, Ranald. You've been hit on the head, so take it slow." Of course, as she was crying the whole time, he wasn't completely reassured.

She went on speaking through her tears. "I need to see if your phone is working." She found it on the hall table and heard the welcome sound of the tone and dialed the castle.

When Aileen came to the phone, Tess sobbed through her explanation. Aileen told her that Hamish was there and would be at the dower house in minutes.

Then she went in search of Duke. "Ye go nowhere without me, m'lady," Ranald said, stumbling to his feet, his voice heart-wrenchingly feeble. "Enough harm's been done."

They found Duke near the road, lying in an unconscious curl of white-and-black fur. But when Tess bent to check, she found a light pulse. She also found the bone to some kind of raw meat wrapped in one of her own sweaters, for scent, she supposed.

Ranald scooped up Duke's body and carried him inside, saying, "I'll take care of the wee pup, m'lady."

"I'll get something for your head." And then she was on her way up the stairs. At the landing she was drawn to the open door of the nursery.

Her feet were suddenly unsteady as she walked into the room. But it was almost as if she had to see if it had really happened. Maybe it had all been some sort of bizarre hallucination.

Her head moved slowly from right to left. There was his chest of drawers, the rocker where she had fed him such a short time ago. And then . . . the crib . . . the empty crib with not even a blanket on it.

The diaper bag was missing too, she noticed immediately after that. Eyes dulled, she went into the bathroom and got the first-aid kit from under the sink.

Downstairs, she saw that Ranald was forcing some concoction into Duke, and the pup seemed to be responding. She opened the freezer for ice and was paralyzed for an endless moment before she pulled one of the plastic trays free.

"They've really taken him," she said, staring at the tray in her hands. "They have my baby."

"They won't harm the bairn, m'lady," Ranald reassured her as Duke squirmed in his arms. "Whatever reason they've done this for, they won't want to harm him."

Blinking hard, she hoped he was right.

Aileen arrived with Hamish. She took one look at Tess's strained white face and pushed her into the den and a chair by the fire. Her own hands were trembling as she poured them both a brandy.

Tess shook her head absently and said, "No. The baby's milk." She covered her mouth with her hand as she realized what she had just said.

Aileen took her other hand and pushed the brandy into it, ordering, "Drink, Tess. Drink it down, now."

Tess obeyed, as people always obeyed sweet Aileen. Finally, she asked, "Is Kyra here? Maybe she can . . . sense something."

"She'll be here in a moment, dear. She's finding someone with a radio to contact Ian." She saw Tess bite her lip. "Then she'll call out the clan."

Tess didn't exactly know what that meant, but it was reassuring. "And Scotland Yard?" she asked absently.

"On their way."

In the next twenty minutes Tess learned what it was to belong to a Scottish clan. Although they'd been at peace for nearly two hundred years, with no more than a single call, hordes of MacLeods came to the rescue. So many, in fact, that Tess was overwhelmed and driven back upstairs.

Hamish had wanted to give her a sedative, but she wouldn't have it. Whatever was to come, she wanted to be awake to face it.

It was on the coverlet of her own bed that she found the crumpled note the kidnappers had left addressed to the Laird MacLeod.

THIRTEEN

Ian stumbled into a madhouse, ablaze with lights and teeming with MacLeods thundering about. But he was through the front door and halfway up the stairs without even noticing. Like Tess, he had to see the empty nursery with his own eyes before he could believe such a horror. But he was stopped at the open door to his child's room.

Tess sat in the rocker next to the crib, clutching a white woolly lamb with a black felt nose Lackie already favored over his other toys.

"Och, love," he said softly from the doorway.

"Ian?" She turned her face toward him with a look both hopeless and hopeful. He saw the streaks of her tears and moved quickly to kneel before her chair and draw her into his arms.

"They've taken our boy," she whimpered into his

thick hair even as she pulled him close in a fierce grip. She needed his size, his strength.

"I ken, lass. But we'll have him returned to us, whatever it takes." He pulled back a moment, searching her face. "Did they harm ye?"

She gave a swift shake of her head, then burst into tears again. "I feel so cold inside," she whispered. His arms held her tight as she cried for a few minutes. She wouldn't permit herself any more—tears were useless. "Give me that handkerchief you always have on you," she ordered her husband gruffly, angry that she had let go.

Ian's eyes were bleak but tender as he pulled the snowy-white linen from his pocket. Och, she all but broke his heart. Sweet thing, she couldn't bear to appear weak.

Tess dabbed at her eyes and blew her nose. Then she reached up into the rocker. "They left a note." She swallowed hard and handed him the paper as if it hurt her even to touch it.

Time slowed as he took the folded white paper gingerly by two fingers. Though he doubted there would be fingerprints, the gentlemen from the Yard would want to check. The letters, sometimes whole words, had been cut from magazines. A dark fury filled his blood as he read it.

Ian MacLeod. One hundred thousand pounds for the package. Tomorrow, 9 P.M., be at the Ky-

leakin pier with the money in a black case and
wait for instructions.

His eyes met hers. "Tell me what happened, can you, love?" He knew he was asking her to relive the worst moments of her life. He wished he had a choice.

She nodded, her deepest blue eyes looking enormous in her white face. Slowly, she began to tell the story, step by step. "They took things for him." She was mumbling now. "Diaper bag, blankets . . . even milk from the freezer . . . breast milk. They took all of it, Ian."

"Dear God," he said in a low voice, and held her tight. Finally, he told her, "I have to go on down now. There will be a great deal of discussion o'er what's to be done, and Scotland Yard will soon arrive and think it's their show alone. We canna have that."

She smiled sadly. "Go on."

"Why do ye not come with me, lass? It might be better to know everything that's being done, don't ye think? Ye dinna want to wait here all alone." He studied her until she finally nodded.

"I'll just wash my face first." She gave a little sigh, and Ian held her cheeks as he pressed a kiss to her soft, swollen mouth. Then he lifted her to her feet.

"Go on, Ian. I'm sure they're all waiting for you. I'll only be a minute, I promise." With one last touch to his beard-roughened jaw, she left him.

Downstairs, Ian found his mother surrounded by the horde, giving orders. There were murmurs of sympathy as he came into the room. Someone pushed a drink into his hand, and he held it for courtesy's sake. He went first to Ranald, who wore a fresh white bandage on his pate.

"How is yer hard head, old friend?" Ian put a hand on the older man's shoulder. He saw the bruise that colored Ranald's cheek, as well.

" 'Tis naught, Ian lad."

The room had quieted, and Ian looked around at his friends and relatives. "Thank you all for coming out as ye have. Ye've heard what happened by now. Unfortunately, we haven't much to go on, only a note. They've asked for money and set tomorrow night for the exchange."

Tess stood at the doorway, then, with Kyra just behind her. He waved them in. "Come, Tess. Kie. I believe ye've met all here." He took Tess's hand in his and laced their fingers together. "I'm thinkin' the kidnappers will be locals. They got through Ranald and into the house too easily to be strangers. Tonight we went to Uig, hoping to discover James Blair and his troublemakers. I believe we were sent out on a wild-goose chase. I've asked Angus to bring Chris MacDonald to us. 'Twas he who gave Uig as Blair's location."

A low rumble swept the room at this disclosure, and then there was a scuffle at the doorway as Gordon

MacDonald and Angus shoved young Chris into the room. Ian felt the fury rise again in his chest, but Gordon started immediately in his booming voice, "I'll tell ye I've had no part of these shameful doings, MacLeod, and that I'm at ye and yer lady's service in whatever way ye like."

Ian studied him a moment as he struggled for control of his temper; then he nodded. "Thank ye, Gordon." He felt Tess stiffen beside him.

"Bring the boy here, Angus," she said, with quiet dignity.

Chris MacDonald was no more than seventeen, and he was shaking in his boots. But Tess had no room for sympathy for him or anyone else who might be involved in the kidnapping. Her only concern was for her son.

Ian snarled, "Do you know what you've gotten yourself mixed up in, Chris? Do you know the penalty for kidnapping?"

"I dinna know what they planned, I swear it! After Jaimie and Fiona's house was burned down, Fiona went on about how someone should be made to pay in pounds for it." One shaking hand swept through his hair. "But they only said the kirk at Uig was one likely spot. They never said for what. After Tim's store was busted up, I thought things were getting out of hand. I dinna want to be involved in more violence, so I went to Angus."

The harsh sound of his breathing was all that was

heard before Tess said quietly, "Come closer. I want to see your eyes when you tell me you had no part in stealing my son, a baby seven weeks old and helpless." Chris stepped closer. "And if you lie to me, Chris MacDonald, I'll find a way to kill you myself with these two hands."

Not a soul in the room begrudged her the threat. But Chris stood straight and tall as he announced, "I had no knowledge of such a foul deed, Yer Ladyship, I swear it. And I'll do anything I can to help you find the dirty bastards." His eyes were clear as they looked into hers, and his trembling had stopped.

Tess took in a long breath and finally turned to Ian. "I believe him," she said.

"And I," Ian agreed.

They questioned Chris for the next hour, first Ian, then the men from Scotland Yard, but concluded he hadn't been privy to the Blairs' plans. They had simply allowed him to be something of an errand boy.

The friends and relatives had been dispersed with instructions to cover the Isle and ferret out any information they could.

Ian was in the kitchen with Tess and Ranald, waiting for the kettle to boil. She had just telephoned her father, who said he would immediately charter a plane from Germany.

Kyra came in and Ian asked, "Anything?"

Kyra shook her head wearily. "I'm sorry. Angus

and I have both been over every inch of the nursery. It's not a thing that can be forced." Ian nodded in resignation.

"There's something I don't understand," he said as Tess poured the tea. They waited. "They must be aware the Yard has been called in on this. How can they hope to make the exchange in full sight of the world on the bloody public pier at Kyleakin!"

No one had an answer.

At four in the morning Ian insisted Tess try and get some rest. She agreed only when he said he would come with her. There was a bit of a bad time when she undressed in the bathroom and found her breasts sore and engorged with milk. She took a deep breath and opened the drawer that contained her breast pump and the attached bottle. When she was finished, she put on her robe and went back into the bedroom.

"Ian?" she asked softly, her lower lip trembling.

He sat on the edge of the bed, preoccupied with the monumental task of taking off his socks. "Yes, love. What is it?"

She looked away. "Can you take this down to the freezer for me?"

Then he saw that she held a bottle of milk, and his throat closed. He could only growl and nod in answer. He didn't know how long he stood in front of the open door of that freezer.

That night, for the first time, he was unable to bring Tess pleasure when they made love. He wanted to stop when he saw the silent tears running down her face, but she urged him on as he slowed, crying, "Please! Yes! Please!" He didn't know that it was the closeness, the feeling of him inside her, that she needed more than physical release. But he would always give her what she asked.

Finally, when he could hold back no longer, he exploded with an agonized cry.

Afterward, she clenched him to her, whispering hoarsely, "I love you. Ian, I love you so much!"

And he kissed away her tears once more.

They slept very little, but when they rose the next morning, they shared their unspoken grief and the certainty that whatever happened, they had each other.

Reports came in all the next day from their people. Every lead was followed, no matter how insignificant it might seem. None proved fruitful.

Janet and Elsbeth both appeared with food and open arms, but Tess sent them out to gather whatever gossip they might, reassuring them that any bit of information could be crucial.

By six o'clock that evening, they had received the cash from the bank and placed it in a black leather case with a minuscule homing device attached to the lining, courtesy of Scotland Yard. Everyone had gathered in the big kitchen.

Ian gave Gordon MacDonald his proxy vote on the bridge.

At half past seven Ian was given a bulletproof vest to wear beneath his black sweater. Then he was given cautionary looks from the females of his family.

The gentlemen from the Yard also had provided repeated instructions about the drop. Under no conditions was he to get into a car with one of the kidnappers. He was to stay within plain sight, and if he recognized Blair, give the signal by brushing his left hand through his hair.

But things weren't to go as anyone planned.

Ian stood on the pier and waited. Minutes ticked by, and he reassured himself that he had been fifteen minutes early. An unexpected chill came with the wind from the bay. He waited. Every sound, every breath of air, and the arrival of each car awaiting ferry passengers drew his attention and that of the six plainclothes agents surrounding him.

Ten minutes after the appointed time, Ian was still staring hard into the rising mist around the pier when he heard the ring of a telephone. His interest was perfunctory until he realized it was the strident sound of a telephone. Pivoting toward the sound, he saw two booths, some twenty feet away.

He took a quick breath and ran full tilt until he grabbed the receiver on the sixth ring. "Yes," he panted. "MacLeod here."

An hour later Ian listened to the sound of the car's engine and leaned his head back against the seat of the government-issue sedan. His driver was a junior officer intent on the road and the rising fog.

He thought of them, waiting at home for him to bring news. He saw their anxious faces in his mind. Tess, eyes wide and hopeful, Aileen, busy with the tea things, anything to keep moving . . . Kyra, talking about whatever she could think of that might distract them, Angus . . .

He sat up with a jerk that startled his driver. "Are you all right, my lord?" But Ian didn't hear him.

Kyra, he thought. Kyra and Angus. But they had tried. They hadn't "seen" anything. Still, his heart pounded and his thoughts buzzed. It was ridiculous. They had no chance at all. He was damned, though, if he was just going to sit and wait to hear that a dead bairn had been found in some hovel!

He turned to the driver and demanded, "Can't this thing go any faster, man?"

"Yes, sir!" the young man answered, and stepped on the gas.

Ian was out the door before the car had even come to a full stop. As he imagined, he found them all in the kitchen.

His urgency was palpable, and they waited for him to speak. Looking into his wife's eyes, he said,

"They've got the money, but the note with Lackie's whereabouts was water-damaged. We couldn't read it. I'm sorry, Tess, they never meant us to have the note. They called me on the pier from the public phone and had me take a launch into the bay—alone." His jaw worked as he struggled to contain his frustration. He saw the light go out of her face and tasted the bitter salt of his helplessness. "The bastard made me swim for it after I tossed him the money. By the time I was back on the boat, he was long gone." Then he turned to his sister with a new sense of purpose. "I know you tried, Kie. I know you and Angus both tried. But I want you to come with me. I need you. Lackie needs you." He looked hard at Angus, and his old friend nodded.

Kyra walked up and put her hand in his. "We'll do whatever you want, whatever we can, *brathair mo.*"

"Good," he said, feeling suddenly hopeful once more. "Come." Then he led them upstairs to the nursery and over to the crib, Tess and Ranald following close behind.

He took Lackie's white lamb from the rocker and handed it to Kyra; the crib pillow he gave to Angus. Then he gestured Tess closer until the four of them surrounded the crib. Ranald stood by the door as a kind of protective sentinel.

"I have no knowledge of when or why your gift works. I have only instinct and a father's love." Tess was watching him and he looked into the endless blue of her eyes. "No one ever loved a child more than Tess and I love Lackie. There must be power in that emotion. Perhaps together, we would have enough power to bring on 'the knowing' in one of you." He looked at each of them and held out his hands, one on either side. "We can try."

So they joined hands and created a circle around the crib, the lamb between Kyra and Tess, the pillow shared by Ian and Angus. Ian closed his eyes and pictured his son, nuzzling at his mother's breast. Tess used the memory of Ian lying before the fire in their bedroom, holding a cooing Lackie over his head. The constant heartache she had known since his disappearance was somehow dispelled by the rich fullness of their love for him. She tried to imagine that the strength of that emotion was, indeed, giving Kyra and Angus a prescient image of Lackie and his location.

Whether it was the sheer concentration of all of their thoughts or something more mysterious, she suddenly felt a rush of energy coming from the hands joined to hers and gasped in surprise. She *felt* Ian's love as strongly as if he were holding her in his arms, and her mind was filled with a kaleidoscope of images of the three of them together.

They waited until time seemed to spin away. Then Kyra began to speak.

"There is an odor." Kyra's eyes opened, and her chin lifted as if the scent were on the wind. "Like damp earth . . . a musty smell . . . and kerosene from a lantern."

Ian felt a wild exhilaration and had to calm himself. It was a place without working electricity. But he needed more, much more, to find them.

"Darkness." Angus spoke in a low voice. "Walls of stone, old walls, hundreds of years." Tess gasped, her throat closing in terror at the thought. Angus gripped her hand harder and continued. "The room is cold. The bairn is well covered against the chill in a basket, but his napkin is wet, and he's fussing."

There was silence.

"Can you see the location? Any landmarks?" Ian urged them at last. But he got no answer. "Can ye tell me more about the room? Are there windows? Is it a shed, part of a house?" His heart clenched, but he had to ask, "Maybe a tomb?"

Kyra answered. "It's one room, and there's a window, but it's been boarded up for a long time. I hear water."

Minutes passed, and Kyra shook her head. Angus still had his eyes closed, but soon he, too, shook his head. They waited. Ten minutes passed, then fifteen.

"No!" Tess cried out suddenly, startling them all as she dragged the hands she clasped to her chest. "It's not over! I won't have it be over!" She trembled, even as she ordered, "Don't you dare give up!" Glaring at Kyra, then Angus, she went on fiercely, "I don't care if it takes all night or all year. I don't care if we stay here until we turn to stone. *You find my son!*"

"Wait," Kyra began, but this time there was something different about her, a kind of certainty. "There's a wheel, and water. It's on a hill, or inside it, I'm not sure." Then her eyes opened wide, and she cried, "Ian!"

His own breath was fast and harsh as he asked, "The old mill, Kie, on the Glendale road?"

"Aye!" his sister answered, and the tears began pouring down her face. Then he was gone.

Kyra knew nothing until she felt Tess shaking her. "Is he really alive? Is he well?"

"Aye," Kyra whispered. "Follow Ian, Tess." And Tess was running through the door, down the stairs.

Outside, Ian was already speeding away in the Saab, but Tess knew the way to the road for Glendale. She had only to find the keys for Ranald's truck.

In a fury of fear and impatience she raced to Ranald's cottage. The keys would be on a rack just inside the door where she'd seen them a hundred times. There! Snatching them from their hook, she ran to the dark truck and yanked the door open.

She took a moment then to catch her breath. She hadn't driven for three long years. But Kyra had told her to go after Ian, and her Lackie waited at the end of that road. She boosted herself into the cab and started the engine without another thought.

Almost immediately, it began to rain. But Tess

needed to catch up to Ian, so she put caution behind her.

Knowing the mill was out of sight around the next bend, Ian pulled onto the turf beside the narrow road and circled round a hillock that overlooked the burn. The rain was driving now. Right behind him, Tess slammed her brakes and followed. Ian was out of the car in a flash, running through the rain to the truck. He wrenched open her door, a tire iron raised in one hand, then he huffed out a quick sigh.

"Ach, Tess! I nearly brained you, thinking you were one of them." Rain poured down his face and dripped from the long red strands of his hair as he leaned in. "The mill's just up a ways; I dinna want them to hear the engine. Stay here and give me fifteen minutes. If I don't return by then, go call for help."

"Don't be an idiot, darling." Tess swung her legs to the ground. "I'm going with you."

Ian stared at his wife for a moment, well aware of her stubborn streak. Then he said, "It's not safe, I don't know for certain what, or whom, we'll find. . . ." She nodded. "All right, then, at least stay here until we know the lay of things." He looked at her earnestly. "Ye will be sensible and have a care, won't ye, lass?"

She hugged him fiercely, head down against his chest. "And you, my love."

Then, with a final buss, he put her from him and started up the path.

The old mill had been a favorite childhood haunt, which is why Kyra had known it. It had been built into the hill some two hundred years before and had been abandoned for at least sixty of those years. Now, it was merely a landmark and a curiosity.

The stream ran down the hill between the paddle wheel and the road, forcing one to cross the burn at the top of the hill and come back down the other side to gain access to the front door. Ian saw that in fact the window was boarded up. When he was a few feet from the door, he heard a radio, and adrenaline shot through his veins. Then he heard the sound of a baby crying. In the next moment he burst through the door.

Fiona Blair stood there, large as life, beside a folding chair holding knitting needless and yarn in one hand. A quick glance around and he saw that she was alone, save for the bairn, crying in a basket next to a portable heater some five feet across the room. She made a move toward the bairn, and Ian warned her, "I've never struck a woman before, but you take one more step toward that basket, and I won't be responsible for what I do." Then he called, "Tess?"

She was behind him, but she had to push at his shoulders to get through the door. "Ian," she said with great impatience and another shove. Her baby was crying. She raced across the room and pulled Lackie from the nest of blankets and up into her arms. Ah, to feel the warmth of his sweet little body again!

She kissed the soft down of his head and murmured endearments. In the background she could hear Ian questioning Fiona.

"Where's your brother? He's had more than enough time to get to ye here."

"What do you mean?" Fiona tossed her head back and tightened her grip on the knitting needles.

"Did ye think I wouldna recognize him behind a mask? Was the ruined note your idea? Just what did you plan for my son, the two of you?"

Tess turned back to them when she heard those words. She stared at the woman who had held her child hostage for all these hours and couldn't even hate her. She was too pathetic, standing there, clutching her knitting, knowing all her plans had come to an end. Somehow she seemed to shrink before their eyes.

"Jaimie's not coming back, is he?" she demanded, ignoring Ian's question. Then she turned to look at Ian directly, and he could see the hatred in her eyes. "You caught him, didn't you?"

Tess held her son a bit tighter as she thought of all that might have happened to him. Ian put the tire iron down on the floor beside him and answered with great calm, "It's over."

She looked down at the bundle in her hand and smiled slightly.

Ian looked at Tess for a moment, trying to warn her with a glance to be ready for anything. Her gaze met his in understanding, and she measured the distance to the door. Ian could certainly take care of himself against a pair of knitting needles, while her own arms were full of Lackie, and he was far too precious to risk.

When Tess took her first tentative step, Fiona raised the needles. Ian grabbed the lethal-looking metal spikes and held Fiona's wrists tight with one hand. Ranald came storming in, followed by the inspector and two of his men.

Ian released Fiona into their custody and Ranald announced that James Blair had been apprehended down the coast a few miles, trying to land the fishing boat he'd chartered.

Tess ignored them completely to rush to her husband's warm arms. She and Ian made a loving shelter for Lackie, and tears streamed from her eyes as she held her family tight. Her heartbeat finally began to calm with Ian's solemn, grateful kiss. He brushed his son's cheek with one finger, and Tess smiled up into his eyes as he whispered her name.

Finally aware of the shuffling of feet, they pulled away and faced the constables. While the details of Blair's chase and capture were explained, Tess finally got a chance to go into a corner and feed Lackie, then change his diaper. She gave him a mother's onceover. He was perfect, emerald eyes sparkling as he blew bubbles and cooed at her touch.

Tess gave a joyful laugh and looked at her husband across the mill. He stilled at the sound, then grinned over his shoulder and winked before he turned back to the inspector.

Tess looked down at Lackie and smiled. "That's our hero!"

Later that night, after a grand and noisy homecoming, Ian took Tess and Lackie away to the honeymoon cottage for a bit of peace. They lay close together on the wide bed, and Ian tightened his arms around Tess. He kissed the top of her head, thinking of how valiantly she had dealt with near tragedy. Aye, she was fit to be wife to a MacLeod chief, and more. There was just one area where she displayed an unwelcome timidity.

"I have been thinking," Ian said as he drew back to see her face. Her eyelids looked heavy. "There's something between us that needs to be set aright yet, m'lass."

"What are you . . . ?" She saw the look in his gemstone eyes and finished with a soft "Oh . . ." Squirming a bit, she looked everywhere but back at him.

"Tell me again."

"What?"

"Tell me!"

"Idiot!"

He waited.

She held out, fussing with Lackie's blanket.

He whistled just to prove that he was still waiting.

She made a "tsking" sound.

He grinned and whistled louder. It was an airy whistle, losing real substance with the laughter.

"Come along, Tess. Or would you show our lad the fine example of your cowardice?" he asked slyly.

"I love you!" she shouted mockingly. Lackie gurgled, and she grinned down at her son lying between them and roundly denounced him as well. "Men! Such an annoyance!" With that, she gathered her beautiful child in her arms and plopped him on his da's taut stomach.

"Oof!" The breath sailed out of him. "I love you too!"

"Good." She smiled a siren's smile and bit lightly at his shoulder. "Then you'll teach me that dance with the sabers."

"Mmm," he answered, thinking she would finally scandalize the Isle, for the sword dance was traditionally performed by the men of the clan.

"Of course," she murmured as she nibbled over his collarbone, "I could always get Angus to teach me."

"And give him a heart attack? Nay, lassie, your adventures are all mine."

She snuggled happily back into his shoulder and ran her thumb over Lackey's soft toes in an absent motion.

"When I get my kilt, there are one or two things I want to change on it," she went on, dreamily. Ian choked and groaned, but she ignored him. "I think I want mine to be just an inch or two higher. . . ."

AUTHOR'S NOTE

The inhabitants of the Isle of Skye will please forgive the liberties I have taken to dramatize this story. Island politics are much more complex than I have represented them. And, although I have used the names of towns and clans, the characters who appear here are completely fictitious and bear no resemblance to those living or dead.

The legend of the Fairy Bridge has been handed down for many generations and is a great tourist attraction on the Isle of Skye. But in the legend, the fairy princess disappears forever. I took the liberty of changing its ending because, like the Lady Aileen, I cherish a happy ending.

Another famous legend of the Isle is that of the *Fairy Flag or Brattiche Shithe*, the clan banner. There are two conflicting stories told of the flag. One is that it was the cloak of the fairy princess and slipped from her shoulders as she ran back to fairyland. The other is that when the nurse of a new MacLeod heir slipped away to the celebration, fairies came to the nursery and wrapped the babe in the silken flag.

It is said to ward off disaster to the clan and, when raised as a battle standard, to make their enemies believe they see three times the number of MacLeods. If, however, it is used more than three times, the flag and its bearer will disappear from the earth forever. The flag has been used twice in battle, leading the MacLeods to victory.

THE EDITOR'S CORNER

Along with the May flowers come six fabulous Love-swepts that will dazzle you with humor, excitement, and, above all, love. Touching, tender, packed with emotion and wonderfully happy endings, our six upcoming romances are real treasures.

The ever-popular Charlotte Hughes leads things off with **THE DEVIL AND MISS GOODY TWO-SHOES**, LOVESWEPT #684. Kane Stoddard had never answered the dozens of letters Melanie Abercrombie had written him in prison, but her words had kept his spirit alive during the three years he'd been jailed in error—and now he wants nothing more than a new start, and a chance to meet the woman who touched his angry soul. Stunned by the sizzling attraction she feels for Kane, Mel struggles to deny the passionate emotions Kane's touch awakens. No one had ever believed in Kane until Mel's sweet caring makes him dare to taste her innocent lips, makes him hunger to hold her until the sun rises. He can only hope that his fierce loving will vanquish her fear of losing him. Touching and intense, **THE DEVIL AND MISS GOODY TWO-SHOES** is the kind of love story that Charlotte is known and loved for.

This month Terry Lawrence delivers some **CLOSE ENCOUNTERS**, LOVESWEPT #685—but of the romantic kind. Alone in the elevator with his soon-to-be ex-wife, Tony Paretti decides he isn't giving Sara Cohen up without a fight! But when fate sends the elevator plunging ten floors and tosses her into his arms, he seizes his chance—and with breath-stealing abandon embraces the woman he's never stopped loving. Kissing Sara with a savage passion that transcends pain, Tony insists that what they had was too good to let go, that together they are strong enough to face the grief that shattered their marriage. Sara aches to rebuild the bonds of their love but doesn't know if she can trust him with her sorrow, even after Tony confesses the secret hopes that he's never dared to tell another soul. Terry will have you crying and cheering as these two people discover the courage to love again.

Get ready for a case of mistaken identity in **THE ONE FOR ME**, LOVESWEPT #686, by Mary Kay McComas. It was a ridiculous masquerade, pretending to be his twin brother at a business dinner, but Peter Wesley grows utterly confused when his guest returns from the powder room—and promptly steals his heart! She looks astonishingly like the woman he'd dined with earlier, but he's convinced that the cool fire and passionate longing in her bright blue eyes is new and dangerously irresistible. Katherine Asher hates impersonating her look-alike sisters, and seeing Peter makes her regret she'd ever agreed. When he kisses her with primitive yearning, she aches to admit her secret—that she wants him for herself! Once the charade is revealed, Peter woos her with fierce pleasure until she surrenders. She has always taken her happiness last, but is she ready to put her love for him first? **THE ONE FOR ME** is humorous and hot—just too good to resist.

Marcia Evanick gives us a hero who is **PLAYING FOR KEEPS**, LOVESWEPT #687. For the past two years detective Reece Carpenter has solved the fake murder-mystery at the Montgomery clan's annual family reunion, infuriating the beautiful—and competitive—Tennessee Montgomery. But when he faces his tempting rival this time, all he wants to win is her heart! Tennie has come prepared to beat her nemesis if it kills her—but the wild flames in his eyes light a fire in her blood that only his lips can satisfy. Tricked into working as a team, Tennie and Reece struggle to prove which is the better sleuth, but the enforced closeness creates a bigger challenge: to keep their minds on the case when they can't keep their hands off each other! Another keeper from Marcia Evanick.

STRANGE BEDFELLOWS, LOVESWEPT #688, is the newest wonderful romance from Patt Bucheister. John Lomax gave up rescuing ladies in distress when he traded his cop's mean streets for the peace of rural Kentucky, but he feels his resolve weaken when he discovers Silver Knight asleep on his couch! Her sea nymph's eyes brimming with delicious humor, her temptress's smile teasingly seductive, Silver pleads with him to probe a mystery in her New York apartment—and her hunk of a hero is hooked! Fascinated by her reluctant knight, an enigmatic warrior whose pain only she can soothe, Silver wonders if a joyous romp might help her free his spirit from the demons of a shadowy past. He is her reckless gamble, the dare she can't refuse—but she needs to make him understand his true home is in her arms. **STRANGE BEDFELLOWS** is Patt Bucheister at her sizzling best.

And last, but certainly not least, is **NO PROMISES MADE**, LOVESWEPT #689, by Maris Soule. Eric Newman is a sleek black panther of a man who holds Ashley Kehler spellbound, mesmerizing her with a look that strips her bare and caresses her senses, but he could also make her lose control, forget the dreams that drive her . . . and Ashley knows she must resist this seducer who ignites a fever in her blood! Drawn to this golden spitfire who is his opposite in every way, Eric feels exhilarated, intrigued against his will—but devastated by the knowledge that she'll soon be leaving. Ashley wavers between ecstasy and guilt, yet Eric knows the only way to keep his love is to let her go, hoping that she is ready to choose the life that will bring her joy. Don't miss this fabulous story!

Happy reading!

With warmest wishes,

Nita Taublib

Nita Taublib

Associate Publisher

P.S. Don't miss the exciting women's novels from Bantam that are coming your way in May—**DECEPTION**, by Amanda Quick, is the paperback edition of her first *New York Times* bestselling hardcover; **RELENTLESS**, by award-winning author Patricia Potter, is a searing tale of revenge and desire, set in Colorado during the 1870's; **SEIZED BY LOVE**, by Susan Johnson, is a novel of savage passions and dangerous pleasures sweeping from fabulous country estates and hunting lodges to the opulent ballrooms and salons of Russian nobility; and **WILD CHILD**, by bestselling author Suzanne Forster, reunites adversaries who share a tangled past—and for whom an old spark of conflict will kindle into a dangerously passionate blaze. We'll be giving you a sneak peek at these terrific books in next month's LOVESWEPTs. And immediately following this page look for a preview of the exciting romances from Bantam that are *available now*!

Don't miss these exciting books by your
favorite Bantam authors

On sale in March:

DARK PARADISE
by Tami Hoag

WARRIOR BRIDE
by Tamara Leigh

REBEL IN SILK
by Sandra Chastain

"Ms. Hoag has deservedly become one of the romance genre's most treasured authors."
—*Rave Reviews*

Look For

DARK PARADISE

by

Tami Hoag

Here is nationally bestselling author Tami Hoag's most dangerously erotic novel yet, a story filled with heart-stopping suspense and shocking passion . . . a story of a woman drawn to a man as hard and untamable as the land he loves, and to a town steeped in secrets—where a killer lurks.

Night had fallen by the time Mari finally found her way to Lucy's place with the aid of the map Lucy had sent in her first letter. Her "hide-out," she'd called it. The huge sky was as black as velvet, sewn with the sequins of more stars than she had ever imagined. The world suddenly seemed a vast, empty wilderness, and she pulled into the yard of the small ranch, questioning for the first time the wisdom of a surprise arrival. There were no lights glowing a welcome in the windows of the handsome new log house. The garage doors were closed.

She climbed out of her Honda and stretched, feeling exhausted and rumpled. The past two weeks had sapped her strength, the decisions she had made taking chunks of it at a time. The drive up from Sacramento had been accomplished in a twenty-four hour marathon with breaks for nothing more than the bathroom and truck stop burritos, and now the physical strain of that weighed her down like an anchor.

It had seemed essential that she get here as quickly as possible, as if she had been afraid her nerve would give out and she would succumb to the endless dissatisfaction of her life in California if she didn't escape immediately. The wild pendulum her emotions had been riding had left her feeling drained and dizzy. She had counted on falling into Lucy's care the instant she got out of her car, but Lucy didn't appear to be home, and disappointment sent the pendulum swinging downward again.

Foolish, really, she told herself, blinking back the threat of tears as she headed for the front porch. She couldn't have expected Lucy to know she was coming. She hadn't been able to bring herself to call ahead. A call would have meant an explanation of everything that had gone on in the past two weeks, and that was better made in person.

A calico cat watched her approach from the porch rail, but jumped down and ran away as she climbed the steps, its claws scratching the wood floor as it darted around the corner of the porch and disappeared. The wind swept down off the mountain and howled around the weathered outbuildings, bringing with it a sense of isolation and a vague feeling of desertion that Mari tried to shrug off as she raised a hand and knocked on the door.

No lights brightened the windows. No voice called out for her to keep her pants on.

She swallowed at the combination of disappointment and uneasiness that crowded at the back of her throat. Against her will, her eyes did a quick scan of the moon-shadowed ranch yard and the hills beyond. The place was in the middle of nowhere. She had driven through the small town of New Eden and gone miles into the wilderness, seeing no more than two other houses on the way—and those from a great distance.

She knocked again, but didn't wait for an answer before trying the door. Lucy had mentioned wildlife in her few letters. The four-legged, flea-scratching kind.

"Bears. I remember something about bears," she muttered, the nerves at the base of her neck wriggling at the possibility that there were a dozen watching her from the cover of darkness, sizing her up with their beady little eyes while their stomachs growled. "If it's all the same to you, Luce, I'd rather not meet one up close and personal while you're off doing the boot scootin' boogie with some cowboy."

Stepping inside, she fumbled along the wall for a light switch, then blinked against the glare of a dozen small bulbs artfully arranged in a chandelier of antlers. Her first thought was that Lucy's abysmal housekeeping talents had deteriorated to a shocking new low. The place was a disaster area, strewn with books, newspapers, note paper, clothing.

She drifted away from the door and into the great room that encompassed most of the first floor of the house, her brain stumbling to make sense of the contradictory information it was getting. The house was barely a year old, a blend of Western tradition and contemporary architectural touches. Lucy had hired a decorator to capture those intertwined feelings in the interior. But the western watercolor prints on the walls hung at drunken angles. The cushions had been torn from the heavy, overstuffed chairs. The seat of the red leather sofa had been slit from end to end. Stuffing rose up from the wound in ragged tufts. Broken lamps and shattered pottery littered the expensive Berber rug. An overgrown pothos had been ripped from its planter and shredded, and was strung across the carpet like strips of tattered green ribbon.

Not even Lucy was this big a slob.

Mari's pulse picked up the rhythm of fear. "Lucy?" she called, the tremor in her voice a vocal extension of the goosebumps that were pebbling her arms. The only answer was an ominous silence that pressed in on her eardrums until they were pounding.

She stepped over a gutted throw pillow, picked her way around a smashed terra cotta urn and peered into the darkened kitchen area. The refrigerator door was ajar, the light within glowing like the promise of gold inside a treasure chest. The smell, however, promised something less pleasant.

She wrinkled her nose and blinked against the sour fumes as she found the light switch on the wall and flicked it upward. Recessed lighting beamed down on a repulsive mess of spoiling food and spilled beer. Milk puddled on the Mexican tile in front of the refrigerator. The carton lay abandoned on its side. Flies hovered over the garbage like tiny vultures.

"Jesus, Lucy," she muttered, "what kind of party did you throw here?"

And where the hell are you?

The pine cupboard doors stood open, their contents spewed out of them. Stoneware and china and flatware lay broken and scattered. Appropriately macabre place settings for the gruesome meal that had been laid out on the floor.

Mari backed away slowly, her hand trembling as she reached out to steady herself with the one ladder-back chair that remained upright at the long pine harvest table. She caught her full lower lip between her teeth and stared through the sheen of tears. She had worked too many criminal cases not to see this for what it was. The house had been ransacked. The motive could have been robbery or the destruction could have been the aftermath of something else, something uglier.

"Lucy?" she called again, her heart sinking like a stone at the sure knowledge that she wouldn't get an answer.

Her gaze drifted to the stairway that led up to the loft where the bedrooms were tucked, then cut to the telephone that had been ripped from the kitchen wall and now hung by slender tendons of wire.

Her heart beat faster. A fine mist of sweat slicked her palms.

"Lucy?"

"She's dead."

The words were like a pair of shotgun blasts in the still of the room. Mari wheeled around, a scream wedged in her throat right behind her heart. He stood at the other end of the table, six feet of hewn granite in faded jeans and a chambray work shirt. How anything that big could have sneaked up on her was beyond reasoning. Her perceptions distorted by fear, she thought his shoulders rivaled the mountains for size. He stood there, staring at her from beneath the low-riding brim of a dusty black Stetson, his gaze narrow, measuring, his mouth set in a grim, compressed line. His right hand—big with blunt-tipped fingers—hung at his side just inches from a holstered revolver that looked big enough to bring down a buffalo.

WARRIOR BRIDE
by
Tamara Leigh

" . . . *a vibrant, passionate love story that captures all the splendor of the medieval era . . . A sheer delight.*"
—*bestselling author Teresa Medeiros*

After four years of planning revenge on the highwayman who'd stolen her future, Lizanne Balmaine had the blackguard at the point of her sword. Yet something about the onyx-eyed man she'd abducted and taken to her family estate was different—something that made her hesitate at her moment of triumph. Now she was his prisoner . . . and even more than her handsome captor she feared her own treacherous desires.

"Welcome, my Lord Ranulf," she said. "'Tis a fine day for a duel."

He stared unblinkingly at her, then let a frown settle between his eyes. "Forsooth, I did not expect you to attend this bloodletting," he said. "I must needs remember you are not a lady."

Her jaw hardened. "I assure you I would not miss this for anything," she tossed back.

He looked at the weapons she carried. "And where is this man who would champion your ill-fated cause?" he asked, looking past her.

"Man?" She shook her head. "There is no man."

Ranulf considered this, one eyebrow arched. "You were unable to find a single man willing to die for you, my lady? Not one?"

Refusing to rise to the bait, Lizanne leaned forward, smiling faintly. "Alas, I fear I am so uncomely that none would offer."

"And what of our bargain?" Ranulf asked, suspicion cast upon his voice.

"It stands."

"You think to hold me till your brother returns?" He shifted more of his weight onto his uninjured leg. "Do you forget that I am an unwilling captive, my lady? 'Tis not likely you will return me to that foul-smelling cell." He took a step toward her.

At his sudden movement, the mare shied away, snorting loudly as it pranced sideways. Lizanne brought the animal under control with an imperceptible tightening of her legs.

"Nay," she said, her eyes never wavering. "Your opponent is here before you now."

Ranulf took some moments to digest this, then burst out laughing. As preposterous as it was, a mere woman challenging an accomplished knight to a duel of swords, her proposal truly did not surprise him, though it certainly amused him.

And she was not jesting! he acknowledged. Amazingly, it fit the conclusions he had wrestled with, and finally accepted, regarding her character.

Had she a death wish, then? Even if that spineless brother of hers had shown her how to swing a sword, it was inconceivable she could have any proficiency with such a heavy, awkward weapon. A sling, perhaps, and he mustn't forget a dagger, but a sword?

Slowly, he sobered, blinking back tears of mirth and drawing deep, ragged breaths of air.

She edged her horse nearer, her indignation evident in her stiffly erect bearing. "I find no humor in the situation. Mayhap you would care to enlighten me, Lord Ranulf?"

"Doubtless, you would not appreciate my explanation, my lady."

Her chin went up. "Think you I will not make a worthy opponent?"

"With your nasty tongue, perhaps, but—"

"Then let us not prolong the suspense any longer," she snapped. Swiftly, she removed the sword from its scabbard and tossed it, hilt first, to him.

Reflexively, Ranulf pulled it from the air, his hand closing around the cool metal hilt. He was taken aback as he held it aloft, for inasmuch as the weapon appeared perfectly honed on both its edges, it was not the weighty sword he was accustomed to. Indeed, it felt awkward in his grasp.

"And what is this, a child's toy?" he quipped, twisting the sword in his hand.

In one fluid motion, Lizanne dismounted and turned to face him. "'Tis the instrument of your death, my lord." Advancing, she drew her own sword, identical to the one he held.

He lowered his sword's point and narrowed his eyes. "Think you I would fight a woman?"

"'Tis as we agreed."

"I agreed to fight a man—"

"Nay, you agreed to fight the opponent of my choice. I stand before you now ready to fulfill our bargain."

"We have no such bargain," he insisted.

"Would you break your vow? Are you so dishonorable?"

Never before had Ranulf's honor been questioned. For King Henry and, when necessary, himself, he had fought hard and well, and he carried numerous battle scars to attest to his valor. Still, her insult rankled him.

"'Tis honor that compels me to decline," he

said, a decidedly dangerous smile playing about his lips.

"Honor?" She laughed, coming to an abrupt halt a few feet from him. "Methinks 'tis your injury, coward. Surely, you can still wield a sword?"

Coward? A muscle in his jaw jerked. This one was expert at stirring the remote depths of his anger. "Were you a man, you would be dead now."

"Then imagine me a man," she retorted, lifting her sword in challenge.

The very notion was laughable. Even garbed as she was, the Lady Lizanne was wholly a woman.

"Nay, I fear I must decline." Resolutely, he leaned on the sword. "'Twill make a fine walking stick, though," he added, flexing the steel blade beneath his weight.

Ignoring his quip, Lizanne took a step nearer. "You cannot decline!"

"Aye, and I do."

"Then I will gut you like a pig!" she shouted and leaped forward.

REBEL IN SILK
by
Sandra Chastain

*"Sandra Chastain's characters' steamy relationships
are the stuff dreams are made of."*
—Romantic Times

*Dallas Burke had come to Willow Creek, Wyoming,
to find her brother's killer, and she had no intention of being scared off—not by the roughnecks who
trashed her newspaper office, nor by the devilishly
handsome cowboy who warned her of the violence to
come. Yet she couldn't deny that the tall, sunbronzed
rancher had given her something to think about,
namely, what it would be like to be held in his
steel-muscled arms and feel his sensuous mouth on
hers . . . .*

A bunch of liquored-up cowboys were riding past
the station, shooting guns into the air, bearing down
on the startled Miss Banning caught by drifts in the
middle of the street.

From the general store, opposite where Dallas
was standing, came a figure who grabbed her valise
in one hand and scooped her up with the other, flung her over his shoulder, and stepped onto
the wooden sidewalk beneath the roof over the
entrance to the saloon.

Dallas let out a shocked cry as the horses
thundered by. She might have been run over had
it not been for the man's quick action. Now,
hanging upside down, she felt her rescuer's hand

cradling her thigh in much too familiar a manner.

"Sir, what are you doing?"

"Saving your life."

The man lifted her higher, then, as she started to slide, gave her bottom another tight squeeze. Being rescued was one thing, but this was out of line. Gratitude flew out of her mind as he groped her backside.

"Put me down, you . . . you . . . lecher!"

"Gladly!" He leaned forward, loosened his grip and let her slide to the sidewalk where she landed in a puddle of melted snow and ice. The valise followed with a thump.

"Well, you didn't have to try to break my leg!" Dallas scrambled to her feet, her embarrassment tempering her fear and turning it into anger.

"No, I could have let the horses do it!"

Dallas had never heard such cold dispassion in a voice. He wasn't flirting with her. He wasn't concerned about her injuries. She didn't know why he'd bothered to touch her so intimately. One minute he was there, and the next he had turned to walk away.

"Wait, please wait! I'm sorry to appear ungrateful. I was just startled."

As she scurried along behind him, all she could see was the hat covering his face and head, his heavy canvas duster, and boots with silver spurs set with turquoise. He wasn't stopping.

Dallas reached out and caught his arm. "Now, just a minute. Where I come from, a man at least gives a lady the chance to say a proper thank you. What kind of man are you?"

"I'm cold, I'm thirsty, and I'm ready for a woman. Are you volunteering?"

There was a snickering sound that ran through the room they'd entered. Dallas raised her head and glanced around. She wasn't the only woman in the saloon, but she was the only one wearing all her clothes.

Any other woman might have gasped. But Dallas suppressed her surprise. She didn't know the layout of the town yet, and until she did, she wouldn't take a chance of offending anyone, even these ladies of pleasure. "I'm afraid not. I'm a newspaperwoman, not a . . . an entertainer."

He ripped his hat away, shaking off the glistening beads of melting snow that hung in the jet-black hair that touched his shoulders. He was frowning at her, his brow drawn into deep lines of displeasure; his lips, barely visible beneath a bushy mustache, pressed into a thin line.

His eyes, dark and deep, held her. She sensed danger and a hot intensity.

Where the man she'd met on the train seemed polished and well-mannered, her present adversary was anything but a gentleman. He was a man of steel who challenged with every glance. She shivered in response.

"Hello," a woman's voice intruded. "I'm Miranda. You must have come in on the train."

Dallas blinked, breaking the contact between her and her rescuer. With an effort, she turned to the woman.

"Ah, yes. I did. Dallas Banning." She started to hold out her hand, realized that she was clutching her valise, then lowered it. "I'm afraid I've made rather a mess of introducing myself to Green Willow Creek."

"Well, I don't know about what happened in the street, but following Jake in here might give your reputation a bit of a tarnish."

"Jake?" This was the Jake that her brother Jamie had been worried about.

"Why, yes," Miranda said, "I assumed you two knew each other?"

"Not likely," Jake growled and turned to the bar. "She's too skinny and her mouth is too big for my taste."

"Miss Banning?" Elliott Parnell, the gentleman she'd met on the train, rushed in from the street. "I saw what happened. Are you all right?"

Jake looked up, catching Dallas between him and the furious look he cast at Elliott Parnell.

Dallas didn't respond. The moment Jake had spotted Mr. Elliott, everything in the saloon had seemed to stop. All movement. All sound. For a long endless moment it seemed as if everyone in the room were frozen in place.

Jake finally spoke. "If she's with you and your sodbusters, Elliott, you'd better get her out of here."

Elliot took Dallas's arm protectively. "No, Jake. We simply came in on the same train. Miss Banning is James Banning's sister."

"Oh? The troublemaking newspaper editor. Almost as bad as the German immigrants. I've got no use for either one. Take my advice, Miss Banning. Get on the next train back to wherever you came from."

"I don't need your advice, Mr. Silver."

"Suit yourself, but somebody didn't want your brother here, and my guess is that you won't be any more welcome!"

Dallas felt a shiver of pure anger ripple down her backbone. She might as well make her position known right now. She came to find out the truth and she wouldn't be threatened. "Mr. Silver—"

"Jake! Elliott!" Miranda interrupted, a warning in her voice. "Can't you see that Miss Banning is half-frozen? Men! You have to forgive them," she said, turning to Dallas. "At the risk of further staining your reputation, I'd be pleased to have you make use of my room to freshen up and get dry. That is if you don't mind being . . . here."

"I'd be most appreciative, Miss Miranda," Dallas said, following her golden-haired hostess to the stairs.

Dallas felt all the eyes in the room boring holes in her back. She didn't have to be told where she was and what was taking place beyond the doors on either side of the corridor. If being here ruined her reputation, so be it. She wasn't here to make friends anyway. Besides, a lead to Jamie's murderer was a lot more likely to come from these people than those who might be shocked by her actions.

For just a second she wondered what would have happened if Jake had marched straight up the stairs with her. Then she shook off the impossible picture that thought had created.

She wasn't here to be bedded.

She was here to kill a man.

She just had to find out which one.

And don't miss these spectacular
romances from Bantam Books,
on sale in April:

DECEPTION
by the New York Times bestselling author
Amanda Quick
"One of the hottest and most
prolific writers in romance today . . ."
—*USA Today*

RELENTLESS
by the highly acclaimed author
Patricia Potter
"One of the romance genre's
finest talents . . ."
—*Romantic Times*

SEIZED BY LOVE
by the mistress of erotic historical romance
Susan Johnson
"Susan Johnson is one of the best."
—*Romantic Times*

WILD CHILD
by the bestselling author
Suzanne Forster
"(Suzanne Forster) is guaranteed to steam up
your reading glasses."
—*L.A. Daily News*

OFFICIAL RULES

To enter the sweepstakes below carefully follow all instructions found elsewhere in this offer.

The **Winners Classic** will award prizes with the following approximate maximum values: 1 Grand Prize: $26,500 (or $25,000 cash alternate); 1 First Prize: $3,000; 5 Second Prizes: $400 each; 35 Third Prizes: $100 each; 1,000 Fourth Prizes: $7.50 each. Total maximum retail value of Winners Classic Sweepstakes is $42,500. Some presentations of this sweepstakes may contain individual entry numbers corresponding to one or more of the aforementioned prize levels. To determine the Winners, individual entry numbers will first be compared with the winning numbers preselected by computer. For winning numbers not returned, prizes will be awarded in random drawings from among all eligible entries received. Prize choices may be offered at various levels. If a winner chooses an automobile prize, all license and registration fees, taxes, destination charges and, other expenses not offered herein are the responsibility of the winner. If a winner chooses a trip, travel must be complete within one year from the time the prize is awarded. Minors must be accompanied by an adult. Travel companion(s) must also sign release of liability. Trips are subject to space and departure availability. Certain black-out dates may apply.

The following applies to the sweepstakes named above:

No purchase necessary. You can also enter the sweepstakes by sending your name and address to: P.O. Box 508, Gibbstown, N.J. 08027. Mail each entry separately. Sweepstakes begins 6/1/93. Entries must be received by 12/30/94. Not responsible for lost, late, damaged, misdirected, illegible or postage due mail. Mechanically reproduced entries are not eligible. All entries become property of the sponsor and will not be returned.

Prize Selection/Validations: Selection of winners will be conducted no later than 5:00 PM on January 28, 1995, by an independent judging organization whose decisions are final. Random drawings will be held at 1211 Avenue of the Americas, New York, N.Y. 10036. Entrants need not be present to win. Odds of winning are determined by total number of entries received. Circulation of this sweepstakes is estimated not to exceed 200 million. All prizes are guaranteed to be awarded and delivered to winners. Winners will be notified by mail and may be required to complete an affidavit of eligibility and release of liability which must be returned within 14 days of date on notification or alternate winners will be selected in a random drawing. Any prize notification letter or any prize returned to a participating sponsor, Bantam Doubleday Dell Publishing Group, Inc., its participating divisions or subsidiaries, or the independent judging organization as undeliverable will be awarded to an alternate winner. Prizes are not transferable. No substitution for prizes except as offered or as may be necessary due to unavailability, in which case a prize of equal or greater value will be awarded. Prizes will be awarded approximately 90 days after the drawing. All taxes are the sole responsibility of the winners. Entry constitutes permission (except where prohibited by law) to use winners' names, hometowns, and likenesses for publicity purposes without further or other compensation. Prizes won by minors will be awarded in the name of parent or legal guardian.

Participation: Sweepstakes open to residents of the United States and Canada, except for the province of Quebec. Sweepstakes sponsored by Bantam Doubleday Dell Publishing Group, Inc., (BDD), 1540 Broadway, New York, NY 10036. Versions of this sweepstakes with different graphics and prize choices will be offered in conjunction with various solicitations or promotions by different subsidiaries and divisions of BDD. Where applicable, winners will have their choice of any prize offered at level won. Employees of BDD, its divisions, subsidiaries, advertising agencies, independent judging organization, and their immediate family members are not eligible.

Canadian residents, in order to win, must first correctly answer a time limited arithmetical skill testing question. Void in Puerto Rico, Quebec and wherever prohibited or restricted by law. Subject to all federal, state, local and provincial laws and regulations. For a list of major prize winners (available after 1/29/95): send a self-addressed, stamped envelope entirely separate from your entry to: Sweepstakes Winners, P.O. Box 517, Gibbstown, NJ 08027. Requests must be received by 12/30/94. DO NOT SEND ANY OTHER CORRESPONDENCE TO THIS P.O. BOX.

Don't miss these fabulous Bantam women's fiction titles

Now on sale

● DARK PARADISE
by Tami Hoag, national bestselling author of *CRY WOLF*

"Ms Hoag is...a writer of superlative talent." -Romantic Times

Enter into a thrilling tale where a murderer lurks and death abounds. And where someone has the power to turn a slice of heaven into a dark paradise.
_____56161-8 $5.99/$6.99 in Canada

● WARRIOR BRIDE
by Tamara Leigh

"Fresh, exciting...wonderfully sensual...sure to be noticed in the romance genre."—New York Times bestselling author Amanda Quick

Ranulf Wardieu was furious to discover his jailer was a raven-haired maiden garbed in men's clothing and skilled in combat. But he vowed that he would storm her defenses with sweet caresses and make his captivating enemy his..
_____56533-8 $5.50/6.99 in Canada

● REBEL IN SILK
by Sandra Chastain

"Sandra Chastain's characters' steamy relationships are the stuff dreams are made of."—Romantic Times

Dallas Burke had come to Willow Creek, Wyoming, to find her brother's killer, and she had no intention of being scared off—not by the roughnecks who trashed her newspaper office, nor by the devilishly handsome cowboy who stole her heart.
_____56464-1 $5.50/$6.99 in Canada

Ask for these books at your local bookstore or use this page to order.

❑ Please send me the books I have checked above. I am enclosing $ _____ (add $2.50 to cover postage and handling). Send check or money order, no cash or C. O. D.'s please.

Name _____

Address _____

City/ State/ Zip _____

Send order to: Bantam Books, Dept. FN136, 2451 S. Wolf Rd., Des Plaines, IL 60018
Allow four to six weeks for delivery.
Prices and availability subject to change without notice.

FN136 4/94

The Very Best in Contemporary Women's Fiction

Sandra Brown

_____	28951-9 TEXAS! LUCKY	$5.99/6.99 in Canada
_____	28990-X TEXAS! CHASE	$5.99/6.99
_____	29500-4 TEXAS! SAGE	$5.99/6.99
_____	29085-1 22 INDIGO PLACE	$5.99/6.99
_____	29783-X A WHOLE NEW LIGHT	$5.99/6.99
_____	56045-X TEMPERATURES RISING	$5.99/6.99
_____	56274-6 FANTA C	$4.99/5.99
_____	56278-9 LONG TIME COMING	$4.99/5.99

Tami Hoag

_____	29534-9 LUCKY'S LADY	$4.99/5.99
_____	29053-3 MAGIC	$4.99/5.99
_____	56050-6 SARAH'S SIN	$4.50/5.50
_____	29272-2 STILL WATERS	$4.99/5.99
_____	56160-X CRY WOLF	$5.50/6.50
_____	56161-8 DARK PARADISE	$5.99/7.50

Nora Roberts

_____	29078-9 GENUINE LIES	$5.99/6.99
_____	28578-5 PUBLIC SECRETS	$5.99/6.99
_____	26461-3 HOT ICE	$5.99/6.99
_____	26574-1 SACRED SINS	$5.99/6.99
_____	27859-2 SWEET REVENGE	$5.99/6.99
_____	27283-7 BRAZEN VIRTUE	$5.99/6.99
_____	29597-7 CARNAL INNOCENCE	$5.50/6.50
_____	29490-3 DIVINE EVIL	$5.99/6.99

Deborah Smith

_____	29107-6 MIRACLE	$4.50/5.50
_____	29092-4 FOLLOW THE SUN	$4.99/5.99
_____	28759-1 THE BELOVED WOMAN	$4.50/5.50
_____	29690-6 BLUE WILLOW	$5.50/6.50
_____	29689-2 SILK AND STONE	$5.99/6.99

Theresa Weir

_____	56092-1 LAST SUMMER	$4.99/5.99
_____	56378-5 ONE FINE DAY	$4.99/5.99

Ask for these titles at your bookstore or use this page to order.